Advance Praise for *Welcome to the Neighbourhood*

"These stories are so sly, funny, and perceptive, it's impossible not to sympathize with the people in them, many hapless victims of their own overthinking, struggling to do the right thing, yet falling face-first into uncomfortable truths about themselves. Clea Young is an astute and compassionate chronicler of contemporary life."

—Caroline Adderson, author of *A Way to Be Happy* and *A Russian Sister*

"*Welcome to the Neighbourhood* is gleaming with insights—hilarious, riveting, quietly beautiful. These stories will sneak up to snare you with their power. Clea Young is an extraordinary observer of life."

—Shaena Lambert, author of *Petra* and *Oh, My Darling*

"A powerhouse collection that delves into the darker side of everyday interactions in the Pacific Northwest, *Welcome to the Neighbourhood* brims with insight and thrums with unexpected danger. In these thirteen taut, riveting stories, Young perceptively explores the lives of characters beset with unexpressed emotions, class tensions, and desires both familiar and strange. With this superb exploration of modern life and the lines people cross, Clea Young proves again she is a master of the short story."

—Saleema Nawaz, author of *Songs for the End of the World*

"This book is a pure pleasure to read! These stories are beautifully constructed and intensely intelligent. Clea Young's prose is confident and precise, and she writes with compassion and clarity about childhood, parenting, and simply being alive during a time of environmental and societal upheaval. This is short fiction at its best."

—Deborah Willis, author of *Girlfriend on Mars*

Praise for *Teardown*

"These stories are elegant, clear-eyed, wry or hilarious, and ultra-attentive to the way we live now."

—Lisa Moore, author of *Caught*

"Clea Young's intelligent stories sparkle with life."

—Zoe Whittall, author of *Holding Still for As Long As Possible*

"Beautifully nuanced, wise, and energetic."

—Miranda Hill, author of *Sleeping Funny*

"Clea Young's prose is nimble, her dialogue smart. This is a remarkable debut."

—Billie Livingston, author of *The Crooked Heart of Mercy*

"Vivid, whip-smart stories about people coping with the perils and pitfalls of modern life."

—Neil Smith, author of *Boo*

Welcome to the Neighbourhood

Stories

Clea Young

ASTORIA

Published in Canada and the USA in 2025 by House of Anansi Press Inc.
houseofanansi.com

House of Anansi Press is committed to protecting our natural environment. This book is made of material from well-managed FSC®-certified forests, recycled materials, and other controlled sources.

House of Anansi Press is a Global Certified Accessible™ (GCA by Benetech) publisher. The ebook version of this book meets stringent accessibility standards and is available to readers with print disabilities.

29 28 27 26 25 1 2 3 4 5

Library and Archives Canada Cataloguing in Publication

Title: Welcome to the neighbourhood : stories / Clea Young.
Names: Young, Clea, 1977- author
Identifiers: Canadiana (print) 20250119668 | Canadiana (ebook) 20250119676 | ISBN 9781487013196 (softcover) | ISBN 9781487013202 (EPUB)
Subjects: LCGFT: Short stories.
Classification: LCC PS8597.O582 W45 2025 | DDC C813/.6—dc23

Cover and book design: Alysia Shewchuk
Cover images: stock.adobe.com

House of Anansi Press is grateful for the privilege to work on and create from the Traditional Territory of many Nations, including the Anishinabeg, the Wendat, and the Haudenosaunee, as well as the Treaty Lands of the Mississaugas of the Credit.

Canada Council for the Arts
Conseil des Arts du Canada

With the participation of the Government of Canada
Avec la participation du gouvernement du Canada | Canada

We acknowledge for their financial support of our publishing program the Canada Council for the Arts, the Ontario Arts Council, and the Government of Canada.

Printed and bound in Canada

For Cole & Jude

Contents

Weekend Guest

Holly and I met because our sons went to the same daycare. It was only when we began talking one afternoon, having arrived at the same time to collect them, that we discovered we'd been neighbours for almost three years.

"Why haven't I seen you at the park or even in the street?" Holly said, while our children flung sand in a corner of the yard. "How is that even possible?"

"Parallel universes," I said. "Missed connections."

In the sandbox her son Ellis's cries became screams. "Excuse me," she said, weaving around abandoned tricycles across the yard. She hauled Ellis onto her hip and began wiping gritty runnels of snot from his face with her shirt-sleeve. "You rabble-rouser," she scolded, even though I was fairly certain it was my son, George, who'd started it.

"Georgie," I said, moving to crouch beside him. "Apologize to your friend."

"He's not my friend," George said.

"I'm sorry," I said to Holly.

"Don't be. Besides, we'll make them be friends."

I was thinking the same thing. We exchanged phone numbers and made plans to get together with the kids.

A WEEK AFTER our first encounter, we were sitting in Holly's kitchen, both kept home from work because of a lice outbreak at the daycare.

"We're opening up the cabin soon," Holly said. "You guys should come up for a weekend. It's more of a shack, really, but it's across the road from a beach."

"We'd love to," I said. It was early in our friendship for this sort of invitation; our husbands hadn't even met. Still, it felt like a given that she should ask and I would accept, that we would want to spend entire days together in the country.

"Day drinking and beach fires," Holly said. "We have our projects, but otherwise—"

"Sounds like paradise," I said.

Holly's home was like ours, a narrow townhouse with many small rooms interrupted by short flights of stairs. On the top floor, the boys tore the bedding from Ellis's mattress and rode it down the stairs. If we'd been at my house, I'd have stopped them. I'd also have put George in a time-out for the sneaky way he kept convincing Ellis it wasn't yet his turn. But we'd never be at my house. I avoided hosting play dates because of George's anxiety. The very mention of inviting another child over, a child who might not respect the order of his carefully arranged toys and colouring books, stressed him out. He often fell apart before his hypothetical friend set foot in our home. Holly didn't care if the kids screamed, fought, pulled the house down around us. It was such a relief. She was a relief. I was secretly euphoric sitting in her messy kitchen, the countertops stacked with unwashed dishes, the floor grimy underfoot. That she hadn't bothered to tidy before we arrived impressed me more than anything. On the rare occasion Alistair and I did invite another family over, I'd spend a few frantic hours scouring the bathroom, vacuuming, and wiping evidence of our dirty fingerprints from the kitchen cupboard doors. When company arrived, I'd pretend we always inhabited this lavender-scented state.

After a while I didn't even register the squalor. I noticed only the prisms hanging in the window as they spun rainbowed light across Holly's make-up-free face, the deep lines emanating from around her eyes when she smiled. She made muddy French press coffee, and I drank two cups even though I knew I wouldn't sleep that night.

Holly had an eleven-year-old daughter, too. She said that because of the age difference, it was like having two only children. She didn't ask why Alistair and I hadn't gone for a second, the question most parents worked up to. It didn't seem to occur to her. Fiona stomped through the door just after three o'clock. She was lanky with tangled, waist-length brown hair pulled behind Puck-like ears. Ratty friendship bracelets cuffed her wrists. Eyes like lemon seeds. She resembled a bitter fairy who'd lost her wings, condemned to live among the less sublime. She kicked off her sneakers, dropped her backpack, then froze at the sound of the boys' voices upstairs.

"They're in my room," she said.

"Oh, Fi, relax. What harm can they do?"

"My stuff," she said, bolting across the kitchen and leaping up the stairs. "Ellis!" she cried. "You're dead!"

"My darling first born," Holly said.

"I'm sure I was the same at that age," I said. Only I wasn't. I would have at least said hello to my mother's new friend; my mother would have insisted I utter some form of greeting, however inauthentic. Fiona hadn't even looked at me, and I felt strangely dismissed. Upstairs, the boys fell silent. A moment later George appeared at my side. He pulled my ear to his mouth, whispered, "I want to go home."

"Don't be scared of her," Holly said.

Above us a door slammed. Ellis began to cry.

"We need more of that shampoo," I said, trying not to itch, certain I could feel nits colonizing my scalp. George frequently threw himself on the floor at the mention of walking three blocks to the drugstore. Today he didn't balk.

"Please," Holly said, contorting her face into a look of desperation. "Don't leave me alone with them."

"You know where we live," I said. "You're always welcome."

As George and I made our way up the hill to the pharmacy,

I tried to remember what Holly and I had talked about all afternoon. Nothing and everything. I'd forgotten the joy that came with finding a match. I'd forgotten what it was to be genuinely curious about another person, to have that person express genuine curiosity about me.

OUR FAMILIES BEGAN getting together for dinner on Saturday nights. We always went to Holly and Sol's place because Fiona often had a friend over, or, if she didn't, she wanted to be in her room with the iPad and her *stuff*.

"You have to admit," I said one Saturday night after a few glasses of wine, "it's rare for the men to hit it off, too."

Sol and Alistair were on the deck making plans to play tennis the next day. I knew Alistair would be hungover and unable to follow through, but it was sweet nonetheless. Holly and Sol's deck looked onto False Creek, a marina of live-aboard boats where I could see dinner parties like ours taking place on the water. It was early June, and although the sun had set, the ocean still simmered in its afterglow. The seawall streamed with a parade of evening walkers. I had always felt a little guilty raising a child in the city, but now I wondered how people in the suburbs could stand it, the isolation, the reliance on a car to get the children to school, to pick up a loaf of bread. But was geography really to blame? Hadn't I, in my high-density quadrant, been as isolated as a homesteader before Holly? Despite sharing walls on two sides,

I exchanged hellos with neighbours only in passing. I might know when they showered, when they flicked on a blender, but I'd never attempted to make a true connection. I only learned a marriage had ended when a moving truck arrived.

Holly stood at the counter spooning mint chocolate chip ice cream into bowls, taking every other bite for herself. I was beyond caring that it was past George's bedtime, that the sugar he was about to consume would add a special layer of hell to our lives. Fiona slid into the kitchen and grabbed a bowl.

"Hey," Holly said. "I haven't seen you all night."

"I have cramps," Fiona said.

"You didn't eat dinner. It's your body saying it's starving."

"So I'm eating." Fiona disappeared back upstairs.

"I don't know how you do it," I said without thinking.

"Do what?" Holly stopped scooping and waited for me to continue. I wanted to say, *I don't know how you keep from smacking her*, but I wasn't that drunk.

"I just mean the whole teenager thing, or almost teenager. They become so guarded."

"Oh, that," Holly said. "She opens up at night in our bed. She talks to me then."

"What does she say?"

Fiona still hadn't addressed me directly, or perhaps she truly didn't see me. Once, when I passed her on the walkway, running over to borrow olive oil from Holly, I said, "Hi Fiona," and she kept going as if she hadn't heard, hadn't brushed within inches of me. What might a girl like that share with her mother in the dark?

Holly shrugged. "Little dramas at school. You know, the usual."

I'd hoped she'd say something that would endear me toward the girl, something that would indicate she was highly sensitive, perhaps, that her rudeness was a cover for shyness or insecurity. I wanted to believe she was less of a brat.

"If only you could tell her none of it matters," I said.

"But it does matter, to her."

"I just mean in the scheme of things, compared to the climate crisis."

"That'll come soon enough. Let her think she's all that matters, at least for now."

I took the bowl of ice cream Holly offered. It was the first time I hadn't agreed with her, the first time I'd judged her parenting. I didn't want to be passing judgment since I loathed that tendency in others. The looks as George burst into a tantrum on a busy sidewalk. The looks as I delivered ultimatums while hauling him off the pavement and eventually settling between him and the curb, where I could protect him from oncoming traffic should he flail in that direction. Holly could feel my disapproval, I was certain. It was obvious in the way I changed the subject, inelegantly, to coyote sightings and disappearing cats.

• • •

THE FOLLOWING WEEKEND we went to Victoria to visit family, and the weekend after that George was sick. I texted Holly to ask if Ellis had caught it. He hadn't; her family was healthy. The conversation didn't extend to when we might see each other again and I felt agitated, at fault.

"I know it's wrong to feel this way about an eleven-year-old," I said to Alistair that night in bed, "but she's just such a snob."

"Is she?"

"Has she said a word to you?"

"I'm not sure I've said anything to her either. We're old people. Invisible. You've got to get comfortable with that."

"How can I like Holly as much as I do and hate her daughter?"

"Hate? Isn't that a bit strong?"

"Okay, dislike."

"Maybe she's picking up on your vibe, the disliking one."

"It wasn't my vibe initially."

"You know you're the adult, right?" Alistair rolled away from me and into a committed sleeping position. A second later he reached back, patted my hip, and offered the advice I didn't know I'd been seeking. "If it'll satisfy your need for revenge," he said, "I can't see any harm in ignoring her back."

I imagined sitting in Holly's kitchen and actively not turning toward Fiona when she entered the room, even though my eyes were always drawn to her—fascinated by her emerging beauty and self-absorption. Fiona wouldn't know the difference, but maybe, as Alistair said, it would give me the satisfaction—fine, the revenge—I craved.

THE INVITATION ARRIVED by text the next morning while I was engaged in the daily battle of getting George out the door to daycare. *Won't go. Hate it.* He wanted to stay home. *Impossible. Work. Must go. You'll have fun.* My phone chimed as he reached peak rage, pulling books off the shelves in his room, his mattress from its bed frame. I was in the kitchen washing dishes, already late for work. When George was smaller, I could physically remove him from the house, strap him screaming into the stroller. But he was too big to manhandle now and I was at a loss. I slammed dishes around in the soapy water, furious at my own impotence.

Cabin excursion next weekend? Holly wrote. *It'll be fun!*

I pulled off my rubber gloves and reread the message a couple of times, parsing it for subtext. I detected nothing. I didn't consult Alistair or acknowledge the thumping sound that had started in George's room.

Yes! I replied. *A thousand times yes!*

It's rustic, Holly responded. *But we'll have gin! And the forecast looks good.*

I drained the sink and took a deep breath. Something to look forward to: beachcombing, swimming, gossiping with Holly. I went downstairs to George's room and faced his closed door. At least he was containing his temper to his own space, just as Alistair and I had asked. We'd even demonstrated what he might do—pound the pillows, pull the duvet off the bed—but this new thing, kicking the bifold closet doors, was all his own.

"George," I said. "Stop. Those are impossible to put back on." He continued to kick, half-heartedly now, and whimper: "My mommy doesn't love me. My mommy doesn't love me."

"Sweetie, you know that's not true." I pushed on the door, but it was blocked. Would he ever outgrow this anger? How would it manifest as a teenager? Would he become violent toward other kids, toward Alistair and me? Would he use drugs to numb his fury? I slid down the wall onto the carpet and waited while he removed the books and toys from the door's path. Finally, he stood before me red-faced and shirtless. I opened my arms, and he crumpled into them.

"Guess what?" I whispered into his sweaty hair. "We're going on a little vacation. We'll sleep in a tent, all three of us."

"Now?" George said.

"On the weekend. But you can start thinking about what you'd like to bring."

"I'll pack my suitcase," he said, brightening.

It was only Tuesday, but the preparations might be enough to get us through the week.

"You must be hungry," I said, and carried him upstairs to start the morning over again.

• • •

WE CAUGHT THE ferry after work on Friday and arrived on the Sunshine Coast under a jawbreaker of a moon. We were giddy at leaving the city and our routines behind. Alistair cranked Bob Marley, and we rolled down our windows as we cruised the quiet roads, coiled thickets of blackberries growing on either side. I swore I could hear honeybees at work. Already I wanted to live there. We could commute to the city for work, I proposed. "Yes!" Alistair said, hitting the steering wheel emphatically. Or we could abandon urban life altogether; we could homeschool George. "Yes!" he said again. "We'll go off-grid, raise chickens and goats!" Alistair and I loved to entertain alternate realities—often going so far as to research real estate and choose our dream home—but we never made any real move to change. I knew we'd spend our lives imagining other ways of existing and end up dying where we were now.

We almost missed the driveway. As per Holly's instructions, the address was scrawled in faded orange spray paint on a boulder obscured by ferns. Alistair turned sharply and parked next to their car.

"It's so quiet," I said when the engine stopped and, with it, the reggae.

"It's dark," George said. "I want to go home."

In fact, it wasn't quite dusk, but the cabin was tucked in among tall firs and their shadows fell like pick-up-sticks around the property. Also, without streetlamps and incandescent lighting from surrounding buildings, it felt as if we'd overshot our destination, landed somewhere deeper and darker than we'd intended.

Across the yard, the cabin door opened, and Holly called out, "At last! Ellis has been climbing the walls waiting for Georgie. And of course Sol and I have been doing the same."

I unbuckled George, and he ran toward Holly's backlit shape, forgetting his reluctance.

"We've set up the tent, so all you have to do is crawl in when you're ready," Holly said. "But I hope that won't be for a while."

Theirs was a ramshackle, two-room hunting cabin, without insulation and utterly charming—the living room shelves stacked with board games and swollen paperbacks, a pair of ironic, miniature wooden antlers mounted above the front door. While George and Ellis jumped between the two sets of bunk beds where Holly's family slept, we drank rosé and ate cheese and olives I'd brought from the city. Fiona was curled up on the couch with a book. She didn't acknowledge us when we entered, so I didn't bother to greet her. Instead, I rambled on to Holly and Sol about our plans to ditch city life and become their full-time country neighbours.

"Ugh, the neighbours," Holly said. "We'd much prefer you guys next door."

Apparently, the property to the east boasted a house worthy of a spread in an architecture and design magazine. Upon purchase, the current neighbours, also city-dwellers, had built a pen for their three pit bulls. Holly had inspected the cage once when she knew they weren't home. "It's sturdy as fuck," she said.

"Mom," Fiona said.

"Sorry, darling. Forgot you were there."

I hadn't forgotten. As much as I wanted to ignore Fiona's furrowed brow, the intensity with which she seemed to be studying the pages of her book, I couldn't help glancing in her direction when I knew the others were looking elsewhere.

"It's cruel to cage them like that," Fiona said. "It's abuse."

"They're rescue dogs," Sol offered.

"Aren't pit bulls known to be unpredictable?" I said. "They flip a switch and turn vicious."

"It's not true," Fiona said, her voice trembling with righteousness. "Only if they're treated badly. If their owners train them that way." It was the first time she'd addressed me directly, except she didn't appear to see me, and she wasn't inviting discussion.

"Your neighbours probably aren't keeping them locked up to be cruel. It's for your safety," I said.

"They do seem a bit wild," Holly said. "But every creature deserves a home. I just wish it wasn't next door."

George was terrified of dogs of all sizes. He leapt into our arms even when he saw one leashed, at a distance. I'd grown impatient with dog owners who felt compelled to tell me their pet was friendly, as if knowing this would alleviate George's fear, a fear that had nothing to do with their precious fur-ball and was perhaps completely irrational, primal, or the result of being bowled over by a rambunctious Labrador when he was learning to walk.

"Don't their jaws lock when they bite?" I said. "Aren't they banned in Quebec?" My comments were for Fiona, but I directed them around the table.

"Anyway, their pen is too small," she said haughtily, rising from the couch.

"My little animal rights activist," Sol said. "She'll be tossing paint on fur coats before you know it."

Fiona stomped past the table and for a moment she was so close I could see a dry smear of ketchup on one cheek and a dreadlock forming at the back of her head. I wanted to point out that the animal lover had just eaten a hamburger. Were cows unworthy of her empathy? Fiona went into the bedroom where the boys were playing. Immediately they stopped jumping and their voices dropped to a hush. My adrenaline spiked; I was poised to charge in and defend them against whatever misdeeds Fiona accused them of: breathing, sweating, laughing. I was practically out of my seat when the circus resumed, Fiona's voice quickly becoming the loudest, most gleeful of all.

THE NEXT MORNING was overcast, but we readied ourselves for the beach as if it were an irrefutable summer day. Holly prepared coffee in travel mugs. "How you like it," she said, handing one to me.

"You're a goddess," I said, and meant it.

She'd pulled her hair into a greasy topknot—grey at her temples—and dressed as though from a costume trunk: water shoes, oversized jeans chopped at the knees and cinched with a ropey belt, and, over it all, a plush, brightly striped bathrobe; shopping at the local thrift store was one of her rainy-day activities. That her appearance was the furthest thing from her mind, or something to have fun with, made her all the more attractive. I felt vain for having brushed my hair and applied chapstick in the tent.

Ellis and George were crouched over a mound of bear scat on the lawn, poking at it with sticks.

"Bears in your front yard and wild dogs next door," I said. "What's next?"

"Occasional cougar sightings," Holly offered.

Sol and Alistair were already out in the skiff, setting crab traps. Fiona hadn't yet emerged from her bunk. Last night, as we'd settled into our tent, George told me he loved her, a declaration I thought he saved for me alone. Apparently, an hour of Fiona's attention was enough to snare his heart.

"I'm glad you had fun," I said.

"No," he said, protesting the dismissal in my voice. "I really do love her."

"That's sweet," I said. "And does she love you?"

I waited for an answer, but his breathing had already lengthened, turned inward. I curled my sleeping bag around his and recalled that brief window before it mattered if a crush returned your love. Reciprocation wasn't the point. It was your own tipsy feelings that thrilled and amazed you.

Holly led the way to the beach, pulling a wagon laden with sand toys, blankets, and snacks down the middle of the two-lane road, bathrobe trailing behind her like the cloak of an eccentric queen.

"Where are the cars?" George asked, and again I felt remiss as a parent, for allowing traffic jams and noise pollution to be his normal.

"I heard the neighbours arrive late last night," Holly called over her shoulder. "Did you?"

I'd woken briefly to a rumbling sound, headlights illuminating the tent for an instant, and then, as suddenly, falling dark.

"I hope they didn't bring the dogs." She sighed.

"Dogs?" George said, yanking my arm and looking up at me.

"They're locked up in a pen," I said. "You don't need to worry."

I wore my bathing suit beneath my clothes, and it chafed in ways I didn't remember from last summer. I cursed myself for not having tried it on before now.

The clouds were layer upon layer of thick flannel sheets that some beneficent hand peeled back gradually, over the course of the morning. Holly and I spread the beach blanket so that we could sit with our backs against a log, facing the ocean's slow theatre: harpy gulls riding the offshore breeze, sailboats flying like spooked mares over the glittering abyss, the retreating tide. The boys played castaways among the driftwood. It occurred to me that I was sitting exactly where, less than a week ago, I'd longed to be: next to Holly at the beach while our boys played without argument. And yet it wasn't what I'd imagined. Panic simmered in my chest, a combination of last night's wine and now the caffeine, but something else, too. I pulled off my sweater and tugged at my bathing suit straps, begging them to lengthen and accept this year's body. I felt oafish and doughy next to Holly.

"Is the water cold?" I asked, rising from the blanket.

"It's the ocean." Holly shrugged. "I plunge when I'm hot." She'd been flipping through a decor magazine and let it drop to the side. I felt her eyes on me as I walked away from the blanket, trying to stretch the bathing suit fabric across my backside and wincing my way over the high-tide line, a mess of sticks and kelp and plastics. Beyond, the tide yawned back to reveal a wide sandy bay. There would be no plunging, only a long torturous entry. My knee joints sang when they finally met the water. I was committed now. Waist-deep, I went under and held my breath. My skin tightened around my bones, and my brain emptied of everything but elemental shock. Sweet summer. Dull bliss. This was exactly what I needed. My reset button pressed. My judgments overturned like buckets of sand. Why should Fiona be polite in the way I wanted her to be? Why wish away her self-centredness? Holly was right; it would be stripped from her soon enough, and wasn't it a mesmerizing study in the meantime? If she did seek my attention, show any sign of deference or interest, what difference would it make? What advice did I have to give? *You are lovely now, but it won't last. Don't squander your beauty, but do share it—with the right people. Don't invest in it because it isn't yours to keep.* No, these were things she had to learn on her own.

I regained my footing and looked back toward shore. It seemed I'd conjured the girl. Fiona had usurped my place on the blanket, head in Holly's lap. My body tingled. Oh, to not have a body. To not care about being seen.

I FLICKED A TOWEL out before me and flopped down on top of it, near the blanket but not so close as to be immediately drawn into conversation. I wanted to be alone in my shivering, salt-stung body and luxuriate in the sun as it penetrated each layer of epidermis until I was warm through to my core. I could hear George and Ellis nattering away, lost in the world they'd created; their voices came and went with the breeze. Even though they were playing happily, I couldn't help recalling what George had eaten for breakfast and estimating how long until his blood sugar crashed. I debated hauling the snacks out of the wagon and calling the boys over to eat, making them eat, but I forced myself to lie still and relax. Fiona murmured something over and over in Holly's lap, maybe a pop song's chorus, and I strained to make out the words.

"I'm bored, bored, so very, very bored," were the lyrics I eventually deciphered.

Holly stroked Fiona's hair. "Oh, Fi," she said. "How can you be bored? Why not walk the beach and explore?"

"Bor-ing."

"Well, what do you want to do?"

"I wish we had Wi-Fi here."

"There will never be Wi-Fi here. Go play with the boys. I'll pay you to babysit."

I wanted to interject, to say the boys didn't need minding.

"You should go swimming," I said. "It's great once you're in."

"How about it?" Holly said.

"My bathing suit's at the cabin."

"Go get it. It'll take ten minutes. Bring the boys and pick some blackberries on the way."

"Will I still get paid?"

"But they're content," I couldn't help saying.

"It'll be good to get them out of the sun for a bit, don't you think?"

"Sure," I relented. "True."

I had no reason to be wary of Fiona, yet I didn't want George going anywhere with her, least of all somewhere I couldn't see him.

"I'm officially on the clock," Fiona said. She put her head down and trudged off toward the boys.

"I want her to babysit for real soon," Holly said. "I give her small assignments when we're here, in preparation. It's part of my grand plan."

"Can she handle both of them?" I said.

"We'll hear their screams if something goes wrong."

I watched as Fiona made her proposition. George's mouth gaped, in awe that he should be the recipient of such an invitation. I caught the words *blackberries* and *magic*, all it took for George to abandon Ellis and take his place at Fiona's side. Ellis was reluctant and required more coaxing from his sister. I trusted his response.

HOLLY EVENTUALLY SHED her robe and went swimming while I affected the look of a woman whose sole purpose in life was to massage sunscreen into every pore of her skin in preparation for hours of uninterrupted napping, reading, and grazing. In fact, I was struggling not to bolt back up to the cabin and spy on the children. What trickery might Fiona be up to? What sly coercions and mind games might she be playing on my gullible child? Holly, poised like an arrow on her back, aimed her stroke out to sea. I could make up an excuse to go back. I needed to pee. It wasn't untrue. But Holly would tell me to go in the water and not jinx our time alone. I opened her decor magazine and flicked at the sand fleas, eager as anyone to inhabit the lavishly countrified rooms. Maybe I just had to acknowledge that letting go was harder for me, the neurotic mother of an only child. Maybe if George had an older sibling, I wouldn't feel this way, I'd have been through it already, as Holly had, and know that the odds of anything going wrong, especially out here in the country, were statistically low.

Holly and I ate crackers slathered in hummus and drank kombucha brewed in her kitchen.

"They're fine," she said, reading my anxiety. "Try to enjoy the quiet while it lasts."

"George has a crush on Fiona," I said. "He told me he loves her."

"That's adorable," Holly said. "Should we try for an arranged marriage? She'll appreciate it in the long run, a younger man. Jesus, would you look at these?" She stretched her thigh flesh taut; clusters of veins sprang in patterns like fireworks across her skin.

"Don't get me started," I said.

"The things that happen to our bodies when we're not looking."

"I *was* looking, and it still happened," I said.

I peered over my sunglasses at the road leading away from the beach and up toward the cabin. I couldn't see anything through the trees. I couldn't hear anything other than waves collapsing, one on top of the other, and my own shallow breath. I flipped to another spread in the magazine.

"Imagine living here," I said.

"With you?" Holly said. "Yes, please."

HOLLY AND I RETURNED to the cabin after about an hour, both of us needing the outhouse and agreeing it prudent we check in. As we trudged up the hill, keeping to the shoulder of the narrow road, I imagined George making the same journey only an hour earlier and miraculously not being struck by a car. I even thanked Fiona in my head for whatever hand she might have had in keeping him safe. The barking was faint at first, but soon it was all I could hear.

"What's that?" I said.

"The hounds of Hades, no doubt," Holly said.

For a second, the bushes on the opposite side of the road shook violently, and then a dog streaked onto the asphalt, its pelt brindled like tiger tail ice cream, a flavour I'd tried once, as a child, and never again. The other two followed in pursuit, and soon three dogs were chasing one another, tongues flapping out the sides of their mouths. They spun an ecstatic circle of tails, then darted in a swift line toward the beach, one occasionally nudging past the other to take the lead. I stood, paralyzed, watching them. They weren't snarling or snapping. I saw no blood on their muzzles. They were clearly playing, but what had they done earlier? George's screams filled my head. He'd been knocked down, bitten. He'd been mauled.

I broke into a run, flesh wobbling, flip-flops slapping. Holly ran, too; I could hear the wagon's brittle wheels jostling behind me. When we turned up the drive, I still couldn't see George or locate his screams, Ellis's too, the back-up singer to my child's headlining hysterics. I only saw Fiona. She was clapping, hopping from one foot to the next, an impish dance that should have been performed in the dark heart of the forest around a bonfire. *You little bitch*, I might have said aloud. George was screaming, "Mama! Mama!" from inside the outhouse. Had he and Ellis run there, terrified, or had she locked them in? Would I open the door to torn limbs? I wanted to shake Fiona by her bony shoulders, force an explanation from her, but I charged past to release her prisoners. The boys were unharmed, outwardly, but George would probably need therapy. He leapt at me, climbed my torso and into my arms. Ellis clung to my legs.

"Nice doggies," I said, trying to reassure myself. "Baby, they're nice doggies. Tell me what happened."

I looked back to where Holly crouched eye-level with Fiona. She held her daughter's hand as if to prevent her running off and spoke in low tones. She was being too gentle with her, too patient. I couldn't help myself. It was the adrenaline. It was my child's contorted face and hiccupping sobs. "You did this on purpose," I spat.

"Did what?" Holly said. Her face turned cold, sharp.

I hardly recognized her. Gone was the warmth, the wry smile and squinting eyes that, until now, had always implied we were on the same team, in cahoots. I didn't bother to elaborate; she understood my accusation, there was no mistaking it, just as there was no coming back from this. I saw Holly and me, our civil avoidance of one another stretched out over the years. Daycare pick-ups, then the elementary school playground, a dance of distance. Neither of us would forget the other's infractions, nor the summer day when the fragile sandcastle of our friendship was trampled as though by a reckless child.

FIONA HAD LED the boys to the pen to show them the dogs were nothing to fear. What an incredible feat this must have been for George, suppressing his dread to do as Fiona—his love—had asked. The dogs had grown excited or agitated or both by the children's presence and began barking and jumping against the fence. This proved too much for the boys and they ran to the outhouse and locked themselves inside while Fiona stayed back, trying to calm the dogs. She only wanted to show the creatures she was gentle and kind, their advocate, possibly even their saviour. This is what I overheard Holly explaining to the neighbours when they returned home to find their dogs missing. She hadn't invited me to be part of the conversation, but I'd tagged along anyway, with my child-appendage whom I was still consoling. But how did they get out of the pen? the neighbours wanted to know. I held my breath as Fiona admitted that, yes, she'd unlatched the gate because they were so frantic. She thought they needed space to calm down.

"You could've been hurt," one of the neighbours said. "Did you not think?"

Silence.

I was vindicated, but it didn't matter.

"They're on the beach," I said from outside the huddle. "They were headed in that direction."

"I'm sorry this is our first meeting as neighbours," Holly said.

"Not her, though," Fiona added quickly, twisting around and pointing at me. "She's not your neighbour." It was the first time our eyes had met, the first time those citric pupils had deigned to absorb me, if only to cast me further apart.

"I'm a weekend guest," I said, though no one had asked. "A city girl, really." The word *girl* soured on my tongue. "Dweller," I muttered. "City dweller."

How would I explain to Alistair, when he and Sol returned, that we couldn't stay? That it was impossible now, and forevermore, to sit across the table from Holly, let alone rejoice in their catch and slurp at buttery crabmeat as if nothing had happened.

FINALLY, GEORGE PERMITTED me to put him down, in his car seat, where he promptly fell asleep. I cleared the tent of our things, then sat near the entrance to the driveway, waiting. After half an hour, Alistair and Sol materialized at the bottom of the hill and began the climb up from the beach. I could tell from the swing in their arms, the lightness of their gear, that they were returning empty handed. I was relieved there was no catch and therefore no carefully considered meal plan that I would be responsible for ruining. But I felt ill over what I was about to interrupt and no doubt quash for good: the conversation rolling between them with such ease, the friendship that had developed, that I'd been so hopeful would take, and had. They were confused to see me sitting there, alone; the looks on their faces were almost sweetly amused. I asked to speak to Alistair alone. It took less than two minutes to detail the devastation.

He was cold to me on the drive to the ferry, insisted on not waking George and remaining in the car even once the boat sailed. I climbed the stairs to the upper deck and let the sun and wind draw tears from my eyes. I thought of what I was returning to, the crowds I pushed through in transit stations, anonymous shoulders and limbs. Con artists, philanthropists, social workers, musicians, politicians, murderers—they were all there. For the most part, until Holly, I hadn't wanted to know my neighbours. I savoured my anonymity. Whenever I visited my small hometown, I was on edge, aware that in the grocery store, the children's petting zoo, the community swimming pool, I might run into someone from my past. There was nothing particularly shameful hidden there, only a girl I'd long grown out of, a girl who believed she deserved more space than others, who swayed her hips when she walked and thought others were watching. And maybe, for a time, they were.

Crows, Kittens, Mint Juleps

We called her Beatrice and knew her only through a third-storey window in the apartment building that looked into Aurora's backyard. We were thirteen that summer before high school and had no idea how old Beatrice was. Sometimes her mother, or a woman we assumed was her mother, would appear in the window beside her. The mother had white hair and a curdled face. She would speak to Beatrice, and then the two of them would disappear from view, or the mother would take Beatrice's place and look down at us, disapproving, in our first bikinis, shoplifted from the Hudson's Bay.

Beatrice had a cognitive disability; I understand this now, but as kids we thought of her as a weird, trapped person who grinned and talked at us from behind glass. We lay on a quilt spread in the uncut grass of Aurora's backyard, torching our young skin, and spoke nonsense to her in return. I could say we didn't know we were teasing her, but on some level, we knew it was wrong to engage with her this way, just as we knew the syllabic aggression of the word *retarded*—a word not yet officially packed away in the trunk of everyday harms—wielded a harsher blow than our casual use of the pejorative implied. I suppose we could have ignored her, and for periods of time, flipping through our *Sassy* and *YM* magazines, we did forget she was there, looking down on us through a window framed in lace curtains, but most of the time we felt her eyes willing us to play. We were still children, after all, and Beatrice, childlike also, presented us with a game.

That same summer, a young man named Raphael moved into a suite in Aurora's house. He had a black-and-white border collie, Freckles, who performed acrobatic tricks, and a guitar covered in stickers advertising the places he'd travelled: Austin, Portland, Dawson, Sayulita. Aurora called him "the hottie," and while I could appreciate that a woman his own age might find his shoulder-length blond hair and beachy blue eyes attractive, I wasn't yet compelled to say such things about a grown man. Aurora's mother, however, wasn't much older than him, and I noticed that if he and Freckles were outside when she arrived home from work, she might linger, pulling dead blooms from marigolds and soaking the two raised beds of vegetables we'd helped her plant earlier that spring.

Aurora's house was divided into four suites, and Raphael's, on the main floor, had a small deck with stairs leading into the backyard. A line cook in a busy downtown restaurant by night, he usually emerged shirtless late morning to throw a Frisbee for Freckles. He'd fling it from his deck and Freckles, crouched and ready in the grass below, would catch it mid-air and dutifully return it to him. One day the Frisbee landed on my back where Aurora and I lay sunbathing in the opposite corner of the yard.

"Sorry," Raphael called. "Wind." To claim there was wind that day, even a breeze, was to have confidence I still don't possess. Freckles appeared beside me, panting, wanting to remove her toy from my body.

"Fetch," I said, and fumbled the Frisbee across the yard.

"If you think about it," Aurora whispered, "he basically just touched your naked body."

"Stop," I said, because I knew Raphael was watching and felt it important to express my displeasure. Even so, I could feel his satisfaction from a distance, in the way he said, "Here, girl," to Freckles, and in the way she obeyed—immediately, with deference—as if to demonstrate his complete control of the situation. He descended from his deck and approached us, shirtless, with a loose-hipped swagger. "Ladies," he said. "I was just thinking ... What if I strung up my hammock back here?" There were only two trees in the yard, a couple of gnarled plums that would soon bomb fruit onto the grass, bringing wasps. Their leaves were our partial shade when the days grew too hot.

"Only if we can use it," Aurora said.

"Naturally," Raphael said. "It's a good one, real comfy."

"Comfy," Aurora said under her breath.

"We'll have to move," I said.

"Why?" Aurora said.

"He'll practically be swinging over our heads."

"It's not that close."

I pushed Aurora off the blanket and dragged it into direct sun. My nose was out of joint, as my mother would say. I'd known what personal space was from a young age. I'd been born knowing and didn't tolerate infringement.

Raphael twisted a large hook into the trunk of each tree and stretched the multicoloured webbing between them.

"This was my bed in Mexico," he said, climbing in and anchoring his arms behind his head. "Wherever I went, beach or jungle."

"Cool," Aurora said.

The exposed tufts of hair in his armpits repulsed me. I pulled a pair of shorts over my bikini bottoms and went inside.

Aurora's home was a wilderness. Her mom rescued plants and animals. That summer she'd taken in an abandoned litter of kittens and a crow with a damaged wing. Tall, glossy-leafed plants acted as stanchions to guide you through the ground-floor apartment. African violets and cyclamen crowded the window sills. The crow barked when I entered. I could hear him climbing the chicken wire of his cage, raking his beak back and forth.

I went into the bathroom and spread aloe vera salve on my pink shoulders. I didn't know how to talk to men other than my father, nor did I have any desire to talk to men outside my family. I knew this was a failing, that my discomfort around Raphael, compared to Aurora's apparent ease, was evidence of my immaturity. But what could I do about it? And why did I have to do anything? I lay on Aurora's bed and lifted one kitten onto my face, set another on my stomach, and held my breath as their claws pricked my hot skin.

IT HAPPENED GRADUALLY. Once, sometimes twice, a week, Aurora's mom, Elaine, would join Raphael for a beer when she arrived home from her administrative job at the Royal BC Museum and before he left for his shift at the "tourist trap," as he called it. She would go inside to change out of her professional attire and emerge in jeans, flip-flops, and a fitted men's undershirt, what Aurora and I referred to as a "wife-beater" without ever considering what those words meant. When Elaine sat with Raphael on his deck, Aurora became sullen and whiny.

"I'm hungry," she'd call up to Elaine. "What's for dinner?"

"You tell me," Elaine would reply.

One day, dragging our boredom through the long hours of the afternoon like a dead limb, we discovered tennis rackets in the communal laundry room, and that evening, while Elaine and Raphael visited on his deck, Aurora kept accidentally-on-purpose lobbing the ball into their conversation. I rallied alone against the fence in a far corner of the yard where there was a pad of cement. At one point I thought to look up to Beatrice's window. There she was, thrilled to have caught my eye. I waved and continued rallying, peripherally aware of the annoyance Aurora presented to her mother. I doubt I would've enjoyed my mother flirting in my presence, either. But I wasn't convinced Elaine was flirting. Neither her voice nor mannerisms seemed altered. She behaved exactly as she might with us, on the couch awaiting an episode of *Unsolved Mysteries* with a heaping bowl of popcorn between us, except she was having a beer with Raphael. Perhaps Beatrice saw something I didn't, though. She jabbed at the glass, pointing to Elaine and Raphael. When I next looked up, she was kissing the palm of her hand.

Finally, one of Aurora's volleys knocked over Raphael's beer.

"Oops," she said. "Sorry!"

"What do you want from me?" Elaine said, exasperated.

"We're starving," Aurora moaned.

Elaine scribbled out a grocery list and gave us a twenty.

"Don't hurry back," she said.

"Funny, *mother*," Aurora said.

We took Elaine's rolling grocery cart because it amused us to wander the aisles like the old women of the neighbourhood. To be clear, Elaine was not an old woman. I've since done the math, and she would have been thirty-two that summer, almost ten years younger than my own mother. But she did not have a car and used a rolling cart for groceries, which made her eccentric. To reach the store, we passed the entrance to Beatrice's building, and as we approached, the woman we thought of as her mother exited and turned in the same direction, pulling her own cart. It was the closest we'd ever come to Beatrice. If we could have sniffed the old woman's hair, rubbed her blouse between our fingers, we would have, just to know the details of Beatrice's home more intimately. Despite her stout frame, she marched quickly, and we had to hurry to keep up. Inside Quality Foods, we surveilled her through the aisles, noting her purchases. The items offered insight into Beatrice's life: bananas, potatoes, raisin bread, ham, yogurt, Shreddies, and digestive tea biscuits. It was thrilling to imagine her mother unpacking the cart before Beatrice's eyes, back in their apartment. We followed her to the checkout counter and watched as she began to unload her provisions onto the belt.

"Touch her," Aurora dared. "Do something."

"Why me?"

"Why not?"

Of course part of me wanted to bridge our gap with Beatrice, to connect with her via the old woman's flesh, even if Aurora and I were the only ones who ever knew such a leap had been made. I reached into the narrow space between her and the grab-rack of candy bars and gum. My hand grazed her forearm. The flesh felt like the pizza dough I made from scratch with my father, airy and limp.

"Excuse me," I said, clutching a Kit Kat. I couldn't meet her eyes when she turned, startled by my touch. I ran.

"If only Beatrice were here, too," Aurora hyperventilated in the aisle of bulk goods.

"Can you imagine?" I said. What might we have done, though? Would we have spoken to her? Or would we have been too shy, too uncertain of how to behave outside our backyard theatre?

We filled our pockets with gummy worms and peppermints from the bulk bins before moving on to Elaine's list: milk, Cheerios, mac and cheese, broccoli. For dessert, a block of Neapolitan ice cream.

AFTER A STRETCH at Aurora's house, we would decamp and move over to mine. I can't recall if this was our decision or the result of a phone call between Elaine and my mother, an agreement to spread the adolescent energy between them that summer. In some ways we had less freedom at my house because my parents, both teachers, were home, and my younger brother, immune to our contempt, followed us around devotedly. What my house had that Aurora's didn't, though, was alcohol.

Weekend nights spent at my house often meant going with my parents to dinner parties that spilled into expansive backyards with speakers perched in tree branches, fairy lights looped through fencing, and self-proclaimed non-smokers hand-rolling

Drum tobacco. That summer there were fortieth-birthday celebrations, bathtubs filled with ice and champagne. There was one party with a makeshift bar surrounded by ferns, behind which a poet mixed mint juleps for the guests.

What did Aurora and I love about being drunk? The feeling of shedding ourselves, bodies that were becoming increasingly confusing to inhabit day by day, not that we articulated it that way. We'd been intoxicated once before, on my dad's home-brew wine, a bottle of which we'd stolen and absconded with to a tent in the backyard. We assumed we'd been stealthy, but the next day the empty bottle appeared on my desk sprouting California poppies, my parents' way of saying they were smarter than us, that they were both amused and not amused.

At this particular party everyone dressed in white. Aurora and I wore peasant blouses and long, full skirts. Our hair fell loose to our mid-backs. We must have looked angelic, virginal, which we were—the latter, at least. What was the poet thinking serving us Bourbon cocktails, two each, with a wink? Around us, partygoers danced to the Fine Young Cannibals in the soaring summer light. A woman stood knee-deep in a koi pond. Aurora and I scurried off to drink our mint juleps in private, beneath an arbour consumed by honeysuckle.

"Disgusting," Aurora said, taking a sip.

"Slam it," I said. It might be the only alcohol we procured that evening. We downed our cocktails and chewed the mint garnish the poet had proudly told us he'd picked himself.

Aurora and I laughed at how our words balled up like small, furred animals in our mouths and refused to come out. We laughed at the stars when they began to appear, how absurdly infinite. We started to feel sick around the time the poet appeared before us.

"Oh, bartender," Aurora said. "Our saviour."

"Your mom's looking for you," he said.

"My mom," I said, and vomited into my skirt.

"Never mind. She's fine," Aurora said. "It's your mint. No good."

The poet might have been twenty, one of the host's students. He had heavily lashed brown eyes and baby cheeks with patchy stubble. The following year he would win an award for a poem about two girls, shit-faced at a garden party. My mother would leave the literary journal in my room, open to the page, and I would feel nauseous again reading it. I wouldn't show it to Aurora because, by then, we'd no longer be close. For my part, I would regret reading the poem, watching the embarkation of my addictive personality through another's eyes, not understanding what I was seeing, or reading, but absorbing its judgment into my bones.

Even in my drunkenness, though, before his poem, I did not appreciate the poet standing over us, the traitorous moon on one shoulder. I was outraged to be at his feet, literally, and grabbed at the cascading honeysuckle, struggled to stand. It was Aurora who reached for the poet's hand. "Help a girl up?" she said. And he did. Of course he did.

My parents indulged our hangovers and didn't speak of the incident for a couple of days. We assumed our behaviour, our tandem bouts of vomiting that continued once we'd been escorted home, had been excused, forgotten. We were wrong.

One evening, Aurora and I lay side by side on my bed, face-masked in Noxzema, when my mother entered without knocking. Earlier, at his request, we'd smeared my brother's face in Noxzema, too, but he'd balked at the tingling sensation—the whole point, we insisted—and immediately rinsed it off. For a second, I thought her visit was about our impatient, uneven treatment of my brother.

"Girls," she said.

We lay very still, staring up at the ceiling. I thought if we didn't speak or move, she might leave.

"You put on quite a show the other night. I don't need to tell you—"

"No," I interrupted. "You don't."

"But I'm going to anyway," she continued firmly.

Aurora's arm pressed alongside mine. It was how we communicated non-verbally, in what we deemed uncomfortable or amusing or inappropriate situations, by pressing some part of our body—foot, hand, arm, leg—into the other, in a way we imagined was invisible to any third party. I'm sure it rarely was.

"You are too young to drink. Way, way, way too young. You're killing brain cells and creating dangerous neural pathways."

Aurora released a sharp laugh, then fell silent.

"It's not funny," my mom went on. "It's actually not funny at all."

I wished Aurora wasn't there beside me. I could handle a lecture from my mom, but I couldn't handle Aurora receiving one, too. She would be livid and embarrassed afterwards, which would leave me no room to feel similar indignation because I would have to defend my mother, out of loyalty.

"We get it," I snapped.

"Do you?" my mom said. "This is the second time."

The chemical bouquet of Noxzema filled my head.

"It won't happen again," I said flatly.

"No," my mom said, "it definitely won't."

She left, closing the door emphatically behind her.

Aurora was silent, seething, I knew. I couldn't bring myself to look at her. We lay still, not speaking, while the room filled with bluish night. I woke sometime around midnight and crept to the bathroom to rinse the dried cream from my face. Aurora appeared in the mirror next to me.

"Horrid," she said, scraping a nail down her cheek. The Noxzema had taken on a yellowish tinge. I handed her a face-cloth. We didn't speak of my mother. We climbed back into bed and the next day moved back to Aurora's house. Usually, I'd ask my parents to drive us, but as punishment—for the lecture, for holding us accountable—we left without a word and walked fifteen blocks.

• • •

THE LACE CURTAINS in Beatrice's window were pulled. She didn't appear the first day or the second. We carried the kittens into the backyard and swung with them in the hammock, climbed the plum trees and ate fruit until we were bloated with gas, lobbed tennis balls at the back fence until we'd lost all of them over the other side. We were bored without her. We missed seeing ourselves reflected in her expressions of delight and surprise. Raphael appeared less, too. We would hear his front door open, the jingle of Freckles' leash and collar, and his footfalls on the stairs, likely heading for the beach at Dallas Road.

"He's ignoring us," Aurora said.

"Who cares," I said.

There was evidence that he and Elaine had spent time together in our absence. On the notepad Elaine used to write messages for us to find upon waking, usually a couple of hours after she'd already left for work, we'd found a draft: *See you around 7.* There was also a video rental beside the door, to be returned: *Sleepless in Seattle.* Aurora's house had no VCR, but we'd heard Raphael mention borrowing a friend's.

"I guess the hottie likes older women," Aurora said. I thought it spoke well of him that it wasn't the opposite.

"Maybe they're just friends," I said.

"I'd want to be more than friends," Aurora said.

Again, we diverged. Was she saying she wanted to have sex

with him? The thought was preposterous to me. It was like saying she was ready to drive to Mexico on her own. Neither of us had even gotten our periods. We had barely-there breasts. It was all talk, but I couldn't even pretend to relate.

"Don't you think he's hot?" Aurora said.

"Not really. He has whiskers." I thought of the brush and cup my dad used to work up a lather for his face in the morning. The expressions he made in the mirror, jutting his chin forward, sliding his mouth to the left and right to make a smooth plane for his razor.

"You're such a prude," Aurora said. "They'd probably tickle in all the right ways."

"You don't even know what you're talking about."

I hadn't called my parents since we'd left in our huff. I knew Elaine would have been informed of our drunkenness, and I thought I detected a tightness from her since our return, clipped sentences, a lack of warmth. Part of me wished she'd get mad at us, too. Instead, she left lists of chores for us to complete while she was at work, which was not entirely unusual, but the lists had become noticeably more extensive: clean the crow's cage, change the kitty litter, wash the dishes, take out the garbage, put in a load of laundry. Summer began to feel like drudgery, and Aurora and I were spending too much time together. Soon, my family would go away for a week to a cottage on a lake. Earlier in the summer, when my mother had told me about the vacation, I'd been anxious at the prospect of leaving Aurora for so long, but now I looked forward to the break. If I could have come up with a good reason to leave her house then and there, I would have. But saying I wanted to go home wasn't reason enough. Aurora would have interpreted it as a betrayal; why would I want to leave her and return to my tyrant mother?

The day we went too far was a Friday in August. We'd been at Aurora's house for nearly a week. It was time for us to move back to mine, but Aurora didn't want to. Elaine returned home from work and appeared disappointed to see us still there. Their apartment was small, a one-bedroom, and the bedroom was Aurora's. Elaine slept on the pullout couch in front of the TV. There was nowhere to escape us.

"Girls, I need a minute," she said.

We went outside and tossed pebbles at Beatrice's window. The curtains remained pulled. Maybe she was away. Maybe she had a summer vacation planned that we didn't know about. And why would we? We knew nothing of Beatrice's life except how it intersected with ours. I wanted to go home. I felt Elaine's frustration and wanted to give her space. All week Aurora had made comments about my mom—how strict, how nosey, how spazzy—which I'd ignored at first, but that became a sore she continued to poke.

"Your mom would've done the same thing," I said finally, fed up.

Aurora bent to scoop a tennis ball from the grass. Then she turned and whipped it at my stomach. "Catch," she said, after the fact.

"Jesus," I said. A welt rose on my bare midriff. It was always a mistake to defend one's mother; it was siding with the enemy.

"Please," Aurora scoffed. "As if that hurt." Then she picked up a stone and tossed it hand to hand like a hot potato.

About half an hour earlier, we'd heard Raphael leave for work, calling words of love and reassurance to Freckles as he shut the door. Aurora eyed me warily, like she knew I was about to turn a corner and was having difficulty seeing what waited, for both of us, around the bend. When she tossed me the stone, I barely held it in my palm before hurling it at Raphael's kitchen window. The sound of rock penetrating glass was chaotic and alarming. It woke us up.

"Holy shit," Aurora said, clapping her hands over her mouth.

Inside Raphael's apartment, Freckles started barking. I turned a slow circle in the yard, as if the last sixty seconds were a skipping rope I could untangle from my limbs. Beatrice caught my eye then, unmoving in her third-storey frame. I could tell from her expression, face scrunched in confusion, that she'd seen the whole thing. Elaine appeared, too; I must have known she would.

"It was an accident," Aurora blurted. She didn't single me out as the perpetrator, but somehow it was obvious. I wore the guilt like jam on a toddler's face.

Elaine hurried up the steps to Raphael's porch and extracted a key from beneath a shell. I saw Aurora considering this detail, while Elaine swept up glass and ensured Freckles was safe.

"I think you should go home," Elaine said when she returned. "You two could use some time apart."

"Mom," Aurora protested.

"Okay," I said. I went inside and found the crow hopping freely around the apartment, the kittens shut in Aurora's bedroom. Elaine often let him out of his cage to exercise his damaged wing, but from the way it dragged at his side it was clear he'd never fly again. My dad answered the phone and I asked him to pick me up, though it was my mom who arrived in the car.

We would leave on vacation in a few days, and I wouldn't see Aurora for the rest of the summer. Neither of us would call the other, even after I returned. I kept imagining the excuses I'd make for not going over, but I never had to use them because she never phoned. In high school that fall we'd say hi, passing in the halls, but no one could have guessed at our closeness just a few months earlier.

My mom pulled away from the curb and turned the corner. We passed the entrance to Beatrice's building, and a little farther down the block, heading in the direction of the grocery store, I saw them walking hand in hand, Beatrice and her mother, which I didn't do with my own mother anymore, but that wasn't the same as not wanting to.

In Loco Parentis

Teja had never worked with this particular boy, a kindergartener named Felix, autistic and non-verbal, a bit of a flight risk. His regular support worker, Emily, was off sick and Principal Langston had asked Teja to step in. This was the nature of the job; you were placed where the need was greatest. Teja's regular morning student required visual prompts and reminders to stay on task, but he would survive without her. Felix, however, could not be left alone. He'd learned to follow routines inside the school, but on the playground, where activities were erratic and unstructured, he darted to and fro, running from loud voices and swarms of children. Oftentimes, he spent the duration of recess with his hands over his ears. Or he beelined for the sidewalk, as if he'd decided, once and for all, that he'd had enough of this charade called an education and was going home. When this happened, Emily had only to take him by the hand and gently steer him back toward the school doors. She had to be watching him, always.

Zipping Felix into his winter coat before they ventured out into the fray of children and weather, Teja recalled something Emily had said in the staffroom recently, that she'd taken Felix once or twice to the neighbouring public playground because it was rarely busy; there he could play on the equipment without the chaos and competition of his peers. And, in fact, once they were outside, he led her in that very direction. It was as if he'd read her mind. *Yes, please, let's leave the riff-raff behind.* The pull of his small hand was so insistent, so communicative, how could she deny him? The public park was separated from the school grounds by chain-link fencing with an opening the width of a doorway, no road to cross, no physical barrier to reach it, but the children knew it was off limits during school hours. Only this was different—Felix was with Teja.

At the foot of the spiderweb, a pyramidic mesh of red ropes that extended about seven feet high, Felix dropped Teja's gloved hand and began scrambling up the structure. He was an adept climber and within seconds sat perched at the top.

"Well done!" Teja said, applauding him. Felix looked off into the distance, expressionless.

Despite the January cold, the park wasn't completely empty. A mom huddled on a bench facing the spiderweb, moored to a stroller, scrolling her phone while a baby slept inside. Another pulled woodchips from her toddler's mouth. There was a hush in the air that felt like snow. Teja walked the perimeter of the spiderweb's base. She pulled her toque down over her ears. Felix wore neither a toque nor mittens, his sensory issues rendering them unbearable. She'd tried, subtly, to raise his hood as they crossed the playground, but he'd pushed it back immediately. She looked at her watch. Seven minutes until the bell rang, summoning them back to the warmth of the classroom. Still, she was happy to be outside. Until recently—before her pandemic-inspired career change—she'd only stepped outside during the workday to get lunch, and only then if she'd forgotten to bring food from home. She'd hardly moved from in front of her computer screen for eight hours. Now she hustled between classrooms and through the halls. She participated in PE if the student she was working with needed assistance, and sometimes even if they didn't. She was exhausted at the end of the day, physically and mentally, but in a good way, a way she felt human beings were meant to be. No standing desk or lunch-hour walking group could replicate the feeling.

"Two more minutes," Teja said. Felix showed no sign of having heard or understood. She pulled a ring with laminated pictures from her pocket—a toilet, a sandwich, a glass of water—and held up the image of a clock in his sightline, in case he glanced down. She wondered if the other women at the playground thought she was his mother, or if they could tell she was a support worker. Above her, at the spiderweb's lookout, Felix held on to a rope with one hand and twirled his opposite wrist, making birdlike peeping sounds at the same time. He was stimming, self-regulating, which meant he was overstimulated in some way, anxious or excited. It was hard to know which unless you had a relationship with the child, had observed him in a variety of situations.

"Felix," Teja said gently, "time to come down." Felix looked off in the direction of the school grounds. The tumult of winter coats and boots was only about fifty metres away, but suddenly it felt to Teja as distant as the moon. She experienced a slight constriction through her chest as she began to realize her mistake. She *didn't* have a relationship with Felix. Why should he listen to her?

Teja manoeuvred to the centre of the web, so that she stood directly below him. "Felix, back to school." On her ring, she flipped to an image of the school, but Felix refused to acknowledge her. She lifted herself onto the first level of rope so that she could reach his foot. She tapped his shoe. "Felix?" She could feel the mom on the bench watching. It was clear, now, that she wasn't Felix's mother. What would Emily do? In the distance, the bell rang, signalling an end to recess. Teja felt unbelievably stupid for having allowed Felix to bring her here, for thinking she could so easily replace Emily, do the things she did with Felix.

Teja reached up, lightly grabbed the shell toe of his shoe and shook it a little. "Fee-lix," she sang. "Hello up there." She could hear the tightness in her voice. No doubt he could, too. He pulled his feet up and away from her. "Oh dear," she said as brightly as she could. The rest of the kindergarteners would be lining up now, waiting for Ms. Lee to collect them and march them back to class for snack time. Teja didn't have her phone with her, so she couldn't even call the office to let them know where she was and ask them to send help. "Okay, Felix, let's go," she sing-songed. Teja watched as he carefully turned around and tried extending a foot to the rope below—"That's it!" she exclaimed—but the rope was an inch too far and he quickly withdrew to his original position. "You almost had it. Give it another try." Too many words. Use shorter directives. "Try again," she said. "Let's go." The mom on the bench lifted her child from the stroller and onto her lap, a baby in a fleecy suit. She wore a frown of disapproval or exhaustion, possibly both.

"It's always easier going up than coming down," Teja said. She remembered visiting Mayan ruins in Chiapas, several years ago now, with one of her kinder ex-boyfriends. They'd climbed a temple's stone steps to an altar where ritual sacrifices were said to have been performed and drank Coke from small glass bottles. When it came time to climb down, Teja couldn't. Her equilibrium balked, somersaulted. The jungle below zoomed in and out of focus. If the temple were a ski slope, it would have been classified a black run. Her ex-boyfriend offered to take her hand, but she only imagined them tumbling headfirst together, like Jack and Jill, two accidental sacrifices to the God of Maize. Teja sat and descended the grand temple's steps on her bum.

How could she convey to Felix that he could trust her, that

he could let go and she would catch him, or, if that was too scary, she could at least guide his foot to a lower rung on the web? The schoolyard was now empty. Soon Ms. Lee would be wondering what was taking them so long. She would call the office, then Principal Langston would come looking for them. Principal Langston was an inscrutable force within the school. She was courteous and fair but utterly unreadable. Teja had overheard stories of after-hours staff shenanigans, drinks at a pub, dancing to a cover band, but her limited imagination couldn't place Principal Langston among the close-knit group of teachers, though she had apparently led the charge to the dance floor. Possibly it was because Teja hadn't yet been fully embraced by the staff that she couldn't imagine socializing with her colleagues outside of school; she was still a newcomer, on unofficial probation. If she was invited to one of these events, would she even go? She wasn't a joiner at the best of times, and people tended to sniff out the antisocial types, attribute to them their suspicions: superior, closed-minded, poor sport. It wasn't that Teja didn't like people or want friends, just that she preferred only a few and in small doses. The school environment was inherently social in its day-to-day functions—wasn't that the real purpose of an education, anyway, to teach children how to function in society at large? But while she found working with kids tiring in a good way, the adult interactions—the small talk in the staffroom, the gossip framed as concern—drained her. It was an ongoing struggle in her life, but one to ponder later.

Right now, her struggle was Felix. Felix off school grounds. Felix unable to navigate the spiderweb. Felix getting colder by the second, but unable to do anything about it, least of all let her know. And her problem was also the mother nursing her fleecy baby, glowering at Teja, weighing her ineptitude. Teja had to agree, she was inept, didn't have any ideas beyond grabbing Felix by the foot and catching him as he fell. Was that wrong, unethical? In her coursework that precipitated this career change, shunting her from in front of a computer screen into the wilds of an elementary school, there was much discussion of ethics. And rightly so. Teja and her cohort would soon be working intimately with the most vulnerable among any school's population. The neurodiverse. There were triggers and sensitivities to navigate. *Connect before you correct*, was the maxim of one of Teja's teachers. *Meet them where they're at*, was another. These phrases ran through her head now. Should she continue to encourage Felix and wait until he figured it out on his own? Should she turn and start walking away? Maybe he would find his footing then and follow. What if he fell and she wasn't there to catch him? In Teja's program they had talked about recognizing your own triggers. Was she unduly worried about getting in trouble from Principal Langston, maybe even being fired? Was she anticipating what the rest of the staff would think of her when word got around, as it always did, that she'd been held hostage at the playground by a five-year-old? Or was she caught up in the more immediate optics of how these random moms at the park perceived her tactics, or non-tactics. Maybe they had a better idea.

"I'd just grab him," the woman scratching about in the woodchips with her toddler said. "He'll fall right into your arms."

"I was hoping I wouldn't have to," Teja said, her words riding a wave of desperation and relief. Relief because this woman, this *mother*, had granted her a maternal privilege she didn't innately possess, to grab one's child in almost any situation, when she felt it necessary for his safety. This mother had assessed the situation and decided it was the best course of action as well.

Felix shifted again at the top of the web, making to stretch his leg for the rope below. He wanted to come down. He was trying to follow instructions. Teja didn't verbalize what she was about to do, she didn't frontload Felix with information like she should have, like she'd been taught, she simply took hold of the small foot dangling above her and pulled. It was over in an instant. The prize was in her arms, flailing about and reaching, trying to grab hold of the ropes—to what, climb back up the web? But she held him firmly to prevent that from happening. One hand caught hold and Teja had to pause and pry his fingers from the rope. She did not put him down until they were through the opening in the fence, back on school property, at which point he turned and tried to run back to the playground, but she blocked him, without putting her hands on his body. He seemed to give in then, or at least understand the game or power struggle had passed. They walked toward the school entrance side by side, two exhausted outlaws ready to turn themselves in.

IT WAS CALLIE, or Ms. Moray, as the students called her, the grade five teacher in the classroom where Teja regularly worked, who texted later that evening to ask if she was okay.

Fine, why? Teja replied.

Have you seen it? Video of you, at work.

Work?

A link arrived next. Callie was Teja's closest companion at school, in part because she was also new, new to teaching, new to the school. They were both riding a steep learning curve in different though adjacent ways and often confided in one another as they tidied the classroom at the end of the day. *Video. You. At work.* Teja clicked on the link. What was she seeing? It was so familiar. Felix atop the spiderweb, herself beneath him. There she was in her puffy winter coat, toque crooked on her head. She was reaching toward Felix, standing on her toes. Then she was grabbing his shoe and catching him tightly—too tightly?—and stopping to peel his fingers from a rope as she tried to manoeuvre out from inside the web. Felix's face twisted toward the camera briefly and Teja's heart stopped. His eyes were wide, brow wrinkled, mouth open in a tight O. And then the video stopped. She played it again. Again. Another text from Callie: *I have a feeling this isn't the whole story* ... But it was undoubtedly a portion of the story, the part where Teja appeared to roughly handle a vulnerable, non-verbal child.

Teja was thirty-five years old. Old enough, some said, to know better; young enough, others said, to learn from her mistakes. Was she a monster, unfit to work with children, as some people in the comments were saying? Teja hadn't thought so, but watching the video on repeat, she wasn't sure anymore. She tried to remember the scenario without the clip running through her head, how she'd experienced it in her mind and body, the feelings of worry, then panic that had surged through her as the clock ticked down toward the end of recess and she realized her mistake. No, she should never have gone to the playground in the first place, but she had, so should she have waited for Felix to find his own way down, however long that might have taken? Some would say yes, absolutely. But what if he couldn't, which was Teja's sense, that he'd gotten himself into a situation and needed help getting out of it. If you can climb up, you can climb down, was the adage. Not necessarily, not always, was Teja's internal reply.

Don't come in tomorrow, Callie wrote. *There might be fallout.*

Teja couldn't respond, but she opened a browser and booked a sick day. *Fallout.* What did Callie mean? A collective shunning? A media circus? Her phone rang with an unknown caller. It rang again. She turned off the sound. The woman with the fleecy baby had taken the video, that much was obvious. Teja had felt her hostility and judgment acutely. The question was, why had she done it? Had she been so disturbed by the scene playing out in the theatre of her local park that she'd just *had* to capture and report it? Teja couldn't believe this was the case. The woman had watched the episode from start to finish, had seen it escalate, had heard Teja's conversation with the other mother, that woman's recommendation to pull Felix down. The woman on the park bench knew the context but had chosen to share only a portion of the event. Why? *Sometimes children need help with their bodies*, one of Teja's teachers had said. That is, if they were engaging in unsafe behaviour. Felix had needed help with his body, hadn't he? He wasn't lashing out at other children, but he'd put his own body in an unsafe position. Teja pictured him turning and carefully extending a leg, trying to reach the rope below. When he couldn't, he'd recoiled into a tight snail of a boy atop the web. He'd needed help with his body; that's why she'd so gracelessly yanked him into her arms when she'd seen the opportunity. But it didn't matter what she thought, in her professional opinion, Felix needed. What mattered was what people saw. And in the ten-second clip they saw Teja's forceful handling of Felix and the boy's frightened face.

Why had she left her siloed administrative job with its passive computer screen and sculpted office chair? Too many things could go wrong when you worked directly with people, especially small ones. And it wasn't as though the pay was better. It was a pittance. Teja's phone lit up. Callie again: *I'm here if you want to talk.* Social media notifications began to crowd her screen. The video of Teja and Felix was embedded in a brief news article she couldn't put off reading any longer.

"She just didn't seem to be in control," Annie McQuaid, a mother from the neighbourhood was quoted as saying. "She was all panicky. Kids pick up on that. That's why he wasn't coming down. He was scared of her." When asked what prompted her to record the incident, she replied, "I'm a parent. If that was my child, I'd want to know how he was being treated, or mistreated, at school." Teja's heart stopped, collapsed, then sped up and tried to escape her chest. Felix's parents. Thus far her brain hadn't allowed her to go there, to stop and ponder the fact that they would also see the video, this snippet of their son's day in which he appeared to be manhandled in a park other than the schoolyard, by a woman who was not his usual support worker.

Teja quickly closed the tab. Whatever else Annie McQuaid said about her ineptitude she couldn't bear to read now. Teja was not a parent, but did she have to be to adequately care for Felix, or for any other child she supported at work? Were her instincts skewed by having never given birth? It was an absurd assumption. She was neither trained nor paid to mother. She had done what she thought was right in an already wrong situation. Teja opened a browser on her phone and cancelled her sick day. She would go to school tomorrow. No point delaying the inevitable.

• • •

TEJA TOOK AN earlier bus than usual and wore a mask, even though they were no longer mandatory. She'd slept fitfully and dreamed of Annie McQuaid and her sneaky paparazzi filming. In the dream, Teja confronted Annie, explained, pleaded. She woke choking on unactualized tears. She hated Annie McQuaid, and gliding down the still dark streets, the bus wipers methodically shunting away the beginning flakes of winter's first snow, she thought to google her and see if she could glean any details about her life. But Annie McQuaid didn't exist on the internet because, Teja determined, she was a pointless nobody, stuck at home with her baby or out roaming neighbourhood parks concocting drama where there was none, or didn't need to be, or shouldn't have been. Fuck Annie McQuaid.

Teja had not responded to any of the social media posts or tags containing the video clip, but she scrolled them obsessively, searching for some indication of her fate. Acquaintances commented: *You think you know someone, True colours, What the actual F@#*!* Others were more cautious: *Is this for real?* She hated all of them for speculating, for not minding their own business, for being so quick to hang her. It was just a matter of time before her own mother logged on and became tangled in the fray.

The classroom doors were still closed and locked when Teja arrived, but she knew Principal Langston would be in her office. Yesterday, she'd been relieved to see Teja and Felix in the hallway when they arrived back at school, nine minutes after the end-of-recess bell; she'd been about to come looking for them. Immediately, Teja explained what happened, about having overheard Emily talk of taking Felix to the public playground, about allowing Felix to lead her there, the stand-off at the spiderweb, and the long wait for him to come down. (She did not include the part about helping him down; she did not think it necessary.) Principal Langston had laughed, said she guessed she didn't need to tell Teja not to be led astray by a five-year-old again. "Lesson learned," Teja said, "and imprinted on my brain for all eternity." It was Teja's first inkling of camaraderie with Principal Langston, whom some of the staff felt comfortable enough to call Sharon. She wasn't at that point, but it gave her hope she might yet.

That hope was dead now. The infinitesimal and possibly imagined headway she'd made with Principal Langston had surely been undone when she'd watched the clip online. *It's not what it looks like*, Teja imagined saying. *It didn't happen like that*. Even if Principal Langston believed her, or was willing to entertain the notion, what about the rest of the staff? Teja had purposely arrived before the crush of her colleagues. The halls were unfamiliar and unwelcoming at this time of morning, before the smell of coffee brewing in the staffroom, the airplane-grade whir of the photocopier spitting out the day's worksheets, and the scuttle of small feet running in to use the washroom before the morning bell. She would miss working here, the community she was slowly becoming part of. But mostly she'd miss the kids.

Principal Langston's office door stood open, as though she'd been anticipating Teja. Her red lipstick wasn't yet in place, nor her mascara. She looked tired, more human than Teja was accustomed to seeing her, still in sneakers.

"Come in," she said. "I tried calling last night. How are you?"

"I don't know," Teja replied. "Not good."

"I have a meeting with Felix's parents today."

"I'm sorry," Teja said.

"It's my job."

"I waited for him to come down, but he couldn't do it. He'd try, but then he'd stop. He was scared—"

"And he looks scared, in the video. Which is what people are reacting to. But they don't know that's his expression generally, even during story time. I know the video doesn't show the whole picture, and I think most reasonable people will recognize that, but there's room for doubt. You're going to have to fill in the blanks very thoroughly."

"I was caught in all those ropes, and he wanted to climb back up. He was reaching for them, trying to grab on, and I just couldn't let that happen again, but now that I'm talking about it, I don't know why. Why couldn't I let him climb back up, or just leave him to figure it out?"

"You wanted to get him back to school. That was the right thing to do. It's just unfortunate you were filmed at that particular moment."

Teja appreciated Principal Langston's willingness to listen to her perspective even if it wouldn't help matters. She'd imagined a harsh reprimand, leaving in tears, but she felt better than she had since Callie first contacted her about the video last night, like she might survive Annie McQuaid's assault.

"I can talk to Felix's parents, too, if you like. If you want me there."

Principal Langston seemed to consider this. An image arrived in Teja's mind then, of Principal Langston on the dance floor, closing her eyes to take in the music and shut out the grubby pub she'd found herself in with her colleagues. If they ever invited Teja, she would join them.

"I don't think that's wise. Not yet." She looked at her watch. "You should go. I'm not sure what this means for your job. That's up to the school board. I imagine you'll be suspended."

Teja thought of the military term *dishonourable discharge*. She would likely receive the equivalent in the education system. It was humiliating and not completely fair. She hadn't meant to hurt anyone, least of all the child whose safety she was entrusted with. And she wasn't convinced Felix had been damaged by the episode. The problem, or fact of the matter, was that he couldn't say how he felt, only she could.

Teja left through a side door. Outside, snow dusted the school grounds. The children would arrive excited. There would be an announcement about not throwing snowballs at recess and, because it was Vancouver, a city at sea level, the snow would be wet, and the children would enter the school drenched and cold without proper changes of clothes. It would be a day of weather management and little class instruction. Some teachers would give in to the excitement and make lukewarm hot chocolate for their students. Others would attempt to ignore the soggy shoes and socks and march through the curriculum regardless. There would be hopeful murmurings among adults and children alike about a possible snow day if the precipitation kept up.

Teja cut through the park and stopped at the spiderweb. She raised a foot onto one rope, then the next, until she sat at the top. It was not so high, not for an adult. The Mayan temple with an altar at the top, where so much blood had been spilled. One minute you're a cow grazing among your herd, and the next you've been chosen as a sacrifice to the gods. Were the gods ever happy, sated? Or did they just lick their lips and want more.

Nest

Don't mess with Marley was a common phrase in the housing co-operative where I was mercifully offered a unit, after several years on the waitlist, the summer my son, River, turned two. Marley didn't mix with the other parents, those supervising their children in the communal courtyard in varying degrees, depending on their child's age. I was out there most evenings and weekends—basically whenever River wanted to play with the other children—but I quickly learned the parent of a seven-year-old might duck inside to get dinner started or throw on a load of laundry. In a way I became an informal overseer of all the kids because I *had* to be out there; there was no turning your back on a two-year-old.

It would be more accurate to say, *Don't mess with Hunter and Koda*, Marley's boys. They were nine and ten and had finally arrived at the top of the food chain. I observed that kids of a certain age—usually eleven or twelve, or those entering puberty—didn't play anymore, opting instead to cocoon with their video games and iPhones indoors. I'd watch them slink back and forth between the nearby 7-Eleven, clutching giant Slurpee cups. Sometimes I'd address them just to make them speak, to remind them they could. But that summer, Hunter and Koda hadn't yet aged out of the courtyard antics. They were full throttle with the water balloons and Nerf guns. They wanted action, and they usually got it because, frankly, they brought it: an energy that accelerated the intensity of play and eventually tipped it over into argument and dissolution. Their presence put parents on edge. If things became unruly, it was understood that whoever had witnessed the trouble would step in and correct the behaviour. Not exactly discipline the children so much as act as referee to their play, and when those boys entered the mix, calling a timeout at some point was inevitable. Marley, though, didn't tolerate orders, not even gentle entreaties of her boys to chill out, if they didn't come from her. And somehow, without ever being present, she heard everything.

Marley's reputation was all gossip until one Saturday afternoon in July. I was outside spotting River as he climbed up and down a set of concrete stairs and shielding him from the limbs of the more sure-footed children flying past. There was some business with bamboo that I was peripherally aware of, children pulling it from the earth and javelin-tossing the stalks across the courtyard. Parents were trying to halt the destruction, threatening to take away privileges like screen time and dessert, none of which had any effect.

The conversation among the adults quickly turned back to what was on everyone's minds: the fugitive boys from Port Alberni, on Vancouver Island. They were teenagers, actually. At first, they were just missing, then, within a matter of days, reports confirmed they'd taken the ferry to the mainland and were suspected murderers travelling north. The news cycle exploded with experts lecturing about alienated boys, violent video games, gender roles, and mental health. We traded sound bites and regurgitated facts about the teenagers' home lives, their parents and community. We speculated about where they'd turn up—relieved that tips from the public suggested they were moving away from British Columbia—and, most of all, why? Why had two childhood friends run off on a killing spree? None among us voiced our real concern, but we all wondered: Could it happen to us? Could our boys turn out like that?

"Dad?" Logan, a tremulous child with long hair and a hysterical fear of squirrels, vied for his father's attention.

"It's always the mothers who get blamed when boys go rogue," said Colleen, my immediate neighbour.

"This goes beyond rogue," said Jake, Logan's father. "It's psychotic."

"You watch," Colleen said. "Their mothers will be burned at the stake."

"Dad," Logan pleaded.

"What?" Jake snapped.

Logan pointed to the playhouse, a wooden gazebo with ferns sprouting from the roof. "They're going to stab us," he said quietly.

Apparently, Hunter and Koda were filing the bamboo stalks into spears to use on the other, less resourceful children. Jake left us to investigate.

"Whoa, whoa, whoa," I heard him say to the boys. "I'm calling a stop work order on this."

That's when Marley appeared, striding out of the shadows. "Watch your tone," she said. I almost let River fall headlong down the stairs. I grabbed his arm, but the yank startled, and possibly hurt him, and he started to wail.

Marley was tall and slender, lean in a way most mothers I knew were not, or no longer. Also stylish, with an asymmetrical bob dyed platinum blonde.

"You deal with your kids, I'll deal with mine," she said, arms triangulated like wings with hands on her hips. I thought of a katydid, camouflaged one moment, transformed into the most striking creature the next. River squawked and writhed in my arms, desperate to begin his obsessive stair-climbing again.

"It's okay, you're okay," I chanted, trying to quiet him so that I could hear what came next.

"This is what kids are supposed to do," Marley continued. "What you're seeing here is natural development." She was calm, composed, but everything about her was taut, trigger ready. I couldn't look away.

"I'm all for development," Jake said, "as long as it doesn't come at the expense of an eyeball." There was an attempt at lightness in his voice, a desire to defuse.

Ignoring him, Marley said to her boys, "Keep it up." From what I could tell they'd never stopped, had barely even registered the altercation over their accumulating arsenal. Marley turned and legged it in her frayed denim shorts back to her place, but not before her eyes landed on me, holding River nearly upside down in my arms.

"Sometimes you have to let them fall," she said, not unkindly. And then she was gone.

"I do," I sputtered to no one. But did I? And why should I? Was she implying I should let River launch himself down ten concrete steps? Was she calling me a helicopter parent? My child was two years old. I couldn't exactly let him run wild with the others, unattended. Strangers often used the courtyard as a shortcut. He was vulnerable in so many ways.

I BEGAN TO LOOK out for Marley, or look for her. I'm not sure which. I brought River outside to play when he was content inside. I imagined scolding Hunter and Koda without cause just to make her appear, to see if she would. I asked the other parents about her, trying to appear casual: "What's that woman's name again?" It turned out everyone enjoyed the topic—*thinks she's better than us, anger management issues, orders takeout seven nights a week*—but no one really knew her.

I did learn the boys usually spent summers with their dad, in Prince George, but for some reason weren't doing so this year, much to everyone's dismay. She was a graphic designer, a runner, but that was it. What more did I want, or need, to know? There were other single moms in the co-op, but she seemed to have it figured out, how to parent and work and move through the world with a fierce, magnetic grace.

I was struggling in my job as publicist for a small local publisher, which often required me to attend events in the evening, necessitating a babysitter. In bookstores, before pitiable audiences of friends, family, and the odd stray, I watched my authors monotone through their self-important work, reading longer than anyone in the room had an attention span for, all while the babysitting meter ticked. I just didn't care like I once had. Whereas I used to view the writing life as sacred, I now saw it as egocentric and my job upholding and promoting it complicit, void of any meaningful contribution to society. But how could I make a change when I had daycare and housing expenses forever bearing down on me? I couldn't afford not to care. One thing I could do, though, was contribute to my new community. It was an unofficial requirement of the co-op that a member from each household join one of the committees that met monthly to discuss and resolve issues related to their mandates—grounds, maintenance, parking, membership, and recycling. I learned Marley was chair of the latter.

The recycling committee's next meeting was in a week's

time, at the end of July. I anticipated it as though it were a date. The evenings were hot, and I was tired from work and my commute, but I was a better mother with something to look forward to. I made watermelon slice and peanut butter toast picnics for dinner, which River and I ate in our underwear on our small sun-splashed deck. I knelt at the tub for longer than I would have liked while he wallowed in the tepid water and ate frozen blueberries. And I let him play outside a little in the evening, even though I didn't have the energy or desire to make small talk with my neighbours at the end of a workday.

"They're in Alberta by now, or Saskatchewan," a dad said to no one in particular, staring into his phone as I hurried along the main causeway, trailing River. I'd followed the updates that day too. The boys from Port Alberni were on the run, moving across provinces, pursued by police. The media was calling it a manhunt. Journalists had descended on their hometown looking to interview anyone who'd ever brushed shoulders with the teens. Colleen was wrong: so far, their mothers weren't being blamed, though their home lives were under scrutiny, particularly that of the boy who lived with his grandmother. There was a story there, a sinkhole in his past from which the darkness sprung. There was less discussion and speculation among the parents as new, grim details were revealed. Three people dead. Communities on edge. The long, glittering days of summer now cast a menacing light.

"Not in the face!" a mother shouted. "No shooting in the face! How many times do I have to tell you?"

I sat on a nearby retaining wall, watching the battle of water guns. River pedalled throughout the chaos in a stray plastic car. The bigger children ignored him, ran past and around him to refill their ammunition at the tap. Hunter and Koda weren't among them, and despite the commotion, there was a sense of ease to the play. Or maybe I imagined it. But no, the parents lingered with their evening drinks out of the line of fire and talked amiably about upcoming camping trips, triple-checking the weather forecast on their phones. There were shrieks and laughter and the odd injustice, but there was no ganging up on one another, no battle to achieve tears, as there would have been if the brothers were involved. One by one the children got cold and tired and were called in. I thought about the troubled fugitives bedding down for the night in mosquitoed wetlands. Were they sick with fear and remorse, or were they exhilarated, triumphant?

"Two minutes," I told River, preparing him to go inside.

Just then Colleen's daughter, Violet, ran past and squirted River's car. I don't think a drop even touched him, but it was the act of being singled out and targeted that startled him and set him crying. Violet ran hooting from sight.

THE CONVERSATION REVOLVED around soft plastics—plastic bags to be precise. Apparently, the city would no longer collect and recycle them. It caused flares of indignity among the five well-intentioned members who comprised the committee. Marley, however, seemed tired as she took notes on the proceedings to share with the board. There were dark circles under her eyes, and her jaw muscles flexed noticeably when a sparrow-like woman named Anne spoke. Marley wore a black tank top and large gold hoop earrings, along with her trademark jean shorts. The door to the common room was propped open to encourage airflow, but only the whoops of children playing rushed in and out.

I had hired a girl whom I'd observed to be one of the least disaffected among my teen neighbours to watch River while I attended the meeting. Her name was Sway and she rode horses on the weekend. Sway was outside with River. I'd instructed her to keep a close watch, to keep him a few steps removed from the play, safe from its volatile epicentre. She seemed to understand. I had not explicitly said, *Keep him away from Hunter and Koda*, but implied it. "Some kids get carried away," I had said, and nodded in the direction of the shirtless brothers whose torsos were scrawled with ballpoint pen depictions of flames.

Anne couldn't move past her dismay over the city's decision on soft plastics. "Why?" she wanted to know. But none of us could say.

"It just means you'll have to take your bags to a drop-off point yourself," Marley said. "It's not the worst thing."

"I'm retired," Anne said, "so I have time to do that. But how many people will?"

"Actually," I said, "I think most people nowadays pack reusable bags. There's definitely growing awareness about the evils of plastic."

"The evils of plastic?" Marley repeated. "Who are you?"

"Lauren," I said, though I'd introduced myself at the start of the meeting.

"No, I know. I just mean, are you some kind of eco-warrior?"

"Sorry?" I said. There was such derision in her voice. I looked around the table to gauge others' reactions, but no one appeared to notice. I grew hot and my face flushed extravagantly. I felt like an ant beneath one of the children's magnifying glasses: seen and deemed worthy of death.

"We'll include this in the newsletter," Marley said. "Maybe put a sign on the recycling room door, too."

The meeting shifted to the need to remind members to crush their containers to avoid bins overflowing before pickup day. Outside, the children's cries were growing increasingly feverish, crossing the line from play into pandemonium. I hoped Sway had hauled River inside by now. I could've gotten out of my chair to look, no one would've cared, but I stayed seated. I didn't want to be singled out again by Marley. Anne continued to wring her hands over the plastic bags and decided she would write a letter to the city. This seemed to calm her. Marley's phone rang, and she glanced at the screen.

"Meeting adjourned," she said, sweeping her notes from the table and heading for the door, phone to her ear. I heard her laugh and felt resentful. Why did I care? Why did I want to befriend the one self-exiled woman in a cooperative? Why not continue to let her drift out there on the raft of aloneness she'd built? I can't say. Only that I felt compelled to lure her in to shore and burn that raft to ash.

IT WAS FRIDAY of the August long weekend and I'd taken the day off work. I must have mentioned it to Colleen because when I woke, she'd already texted, suggesting we have coffee on the communal deck. Colleen was the best sort of neighbour: welcoming, unobtrusive, chatty. But I didn't want to be her friend, her confidante. I had no desire to map her quirks and failings the way I did Marley's. Colleen gave me everything up front, laid it all out there like garage sale treasures on quilts for every passerby to observe and comment on. I did not covet those kinds of treasures. I wanted a small glass swan slipped to me in the night or beneath a table, and to know it was only mine to hold. Still, I texted Colleen back and told her I'd join her in twenty minutes after River's breakfast.

"All we want is for our sons to become good men, am I right?" Colleen launched in as soon as I was across from her at the picnic table. "But how, exactly, do we do this when the patriarchy's been pinching our asses since we were choosing penny candies at the corner store? That's just my experience. I don't know about you," she said, not waiting for a reply. "It should really be *#mefuckingtoo* because, honestly, how is this a revelation to anyone? And, more importantly, considering how we came up, are we even equipped to guide our twenty-first-century boys?"

A wasp zipped around my mug, and I swatted it away. "Good question," I said. I wasn't prepared for pre-coffee philosophizing.

"I like that you don't cut his hair," Colleen said, nodding toward where River was making his way in the direction of the sandbox we all knew was filled with cat feces.

"River," I said to his small, determined back, "not in there, please."

"Why do we cut boys' hair and let girls' grow long? It's so stupid, but it's a perfect example of one of those things we don't think about. Though clearly you do."

There was a wasp in my coffee now, and I tried to tip it into a potted hosta without losing it all. "I'm not sure I do," I said, watching the wasp crawl about in the dirt. "I just think he has amazing hair."

"Well, whatever," Colleen said. "You're doing a great job."

"Thanks," I said. "We're all just muddling along, aren't we, hoping to get some of it right?"

"Some of us think we have it all figured out." Colleen rolled her eyes in the direction of Marley's place, where I could see the sliding glass door was open, a gauzy curtain catching the breeze. "She could learn a thing or two from you."

"I'm not so sure about that," I said.

Other doors began to open; children trickled out with unbrushed hair, eyes pinched against the sun. River was now digging with commitment in the sandbox and I didn't have the heart to stop him, cat feces or not, because I was drinking my coffee in peace.

"There must be a nest somewhere," Colleen said, flapping her hands and rising suddenly so that the picnic table rocked and more of my coffee spilled. "It happens every year."

I HAD PLANS TO take River to the spray park on Granville Island, but the day kept getting away from me. After the sandbox he was tired and went down for a nap. While he slept, I answered a few emails, one from an author anxious for me to post a positive review of her work on social media before it became old news, another who'd found a misplaced comma in her biography on the publisher's website. *Who's going to notice?* I wanted to reply, but instead I corrected it, let her know I'd done so, and thanked her for her keen eye. I filled a tray of juice popsicles and put them in the freezer, fished flies from the inflatable wading pool I'd set up on our deck, and added some fresh water.

But when River woke, he had a low fever. I tried to carry him to the pool, but he thrashed and moaned, so I abandoned the idea and gave him a dose of Tylenol instead. He fell asleep again and I saw our long weekend plans—beach jaunts and ice cream stops—crumble into a rubble of indistinct hours spent nursing River's symptoms and streaming movies. I had no official summer vacation planned; I didn't have the money.

And while I could've arranged to visit my father and his wife in the Okanagan, we'd have to bus both ways and be subjected to the fierce orderliness of their lake-view condo. The thought of keeping my sticky, cherry-juice-stained child off their white couches did not sound like a vacation.

Later that afternoon, River sat naked in my lap while I fed him green Jell-O. He took small, unenthusiastic bites, and I wondered if I should take him to emergency at Children's Hospital. His body burned against mine, and he shivered violently when I held a cold cloth to his forehead. He'd had colds in the past, many snotty faced colds, but this was new for me. He couldn't even keep his eyes open for *Paw Patrol*.

I heard parents outside, a discharge of laughter followed by a shout of reprimand. With River asleep again, I checked the news on my phone. An aluminum boat, presumed to have been used by the outlaw teens, had been found on the banks of the Nelson River in Manitoba. Small communities in the area were setting curfews. The boggy forest along the river was too dense for a ground search, so helicopters beat the air overhead, trying to flush them out. I looked at River's small shape under the sheet. How did a boy go wrong? How to know when he's taken a fork in the road and call him back before it's too late? The sheet rose and fell with his breath. I put my face to his mouth to smell the hot, sugary life in him.

Colleen texted to invite me outside for a glass of wine. I told her about River, and she said we could sit near my place with the door open, so I could hear if he needed me. I said

I had a headache and didn't think I could drink wine. She replied I could drink whatever I liked. I could think of no other excuse, so I took a glass of water outside to join her. The evening glowed with false promise that August would never end, that we would never again find ourselves in the grip of November rain. Colleen had told me it happened almost like clockwork in the co-op; come October, the doors closed and hibernation began. I wouldn't see most of my neighbours again until May. I welcomed the prospect of seclusion, quiet, but I also would have liked to have a friend nearby with whom I didn't need to make plans, who might just knock on my door and visit for an hour. I imagined Marley dropping by with sushi, eating with her amid the containers at my felt-pen-stained kitchen table while snow fell outside.

"Should I be worried?" I said.

"Kids get sick all the time," Colleen said. "He picked something up at daycare." She had two kids, a pre-teen boy and six-year-old Violet, one of the few girls roaming the co-op. When she spoke of them, or about children in general, it was with a weary knowledge that came from experience, and while she tended to set my mind at ease, she also shut down any discussion. There wasn't room for possibility with Colleen.

The water guns were out that evening, and from where we sat, I could see long arcs shoot skyward, into trees and over railings onto my neighbours' deck chairs. The children weren't background noise tonight; they were warriors on a mission. Hunter and Koda were whipping up a frenzy, calling for teams, for battle.

"When they catch those boys, I hope they're locked up and psychoanalyzed," Colleen said. "I want to see brain scans and pictures of their bedrooms, the posters on their walls and the books on their shelves. The whole story's there, we're just not hearing it."

"It has to end soon," I said. "They're going to get caught."

"Of course they will. Teenagers are notoriously stupid."

A cluster of parents were seated on a deck a little ways down from us, closer to the action. I wanted Colleen to join them, the livelier group. I wanted to go inside and imagine another life for myself and River, searching out vocational programs on college websites. Or I wanted to watch Netflix. I didn't want to think about those messed-up boys on the run.

When they were found, a couple days later, they would be dead, killed by their own or each other's hand. The videos they recorded before their deaths wouldn't be made public. And the public would gladly forget about them and the working-class mill town that made them. Their mothers would never be interviewed. Their mothers wouldn't surface, either, out of grief or horror or non-existence. What could they have said? What could they have done?

I gulped my water and said I needed to check on River. "I might be a while."

"I'll be here," Colleen said. "Violet's down there in the mayhem, so I'm not going anywhere."

Inside, River had kicked off his sheet and lay breathing steadily. His forehead was still hot to the touch. I kissed his cheeks and his arm flung up involuntarily. He moaned, rolled onto his stomach. I scanned his back, legs, feet. Something caught my eye. On his soles: spots, pinpricks of red. I searched the rest of his body and found them on his palms, too. I pulled out my phone and googled: *fever spots on hands and feet*. Apparently, River had a common virus among preschool-age children: hand, foot, and mouth disease. The spots would swell into tiny blisters, and there were likely more percolating on the insides of his cheeks and on his tongue. I was relieved. Colleen was right: something he picked up at daycare. I pulled the fan from the closet and set it at the foot of the bed, wind rippling across the sheets. I was not an incompetent mother, only inexperienced. I needed people like Colleen in my life. She didn't have to be my best friend, just a friend. Did people even have best friends past a certain age? Generally, that was someone's partner, but River's father and I had messed that up, luckily before River was born.

When I returned outside Colleen was gone. So was the other group of parents who'd gathered farther down the row. Had I been inside that long? Surely everyone's dinner hadn't arrived at the same moment. I heard traffic on the neighbouring street, an indicator of the absence of children's cries. A stream of water shot up into the giant maple that shaded the sandbox and gazebo. The water arced and broke apart in silvery chunks as it fell back to earth. Then another stream, another. No, they were two separate streams. Two water guns aiming at the same target. I moved closer to see what they were so bent on hitting.

"Knock it off, you guys," I heard someone say. A woman. "We'll need an ambulance if you keep this up."

The streams of water continued, synchronous, deliberate, reaching for what I finally saw was a large grey cone fixed to a high branch. A wasp nest. I moved to the stairs leading down into the courtyard. From there I saw Hunter and Koda, side by side, water bazookas in hand, determined to shoot it down. I understood the appeal, the desire to watch it fall and detonate on the pavement below, an explosion of wasps.

"People are allergic," Marley said to her boys' resolute backs. "You two, *enough*."

The streams of water continued. The nest rocked a little. They were only managing to hit the bottom, the wasps' entrance, and I could see a small swarm gathering at the opening.

"So, no video games for a week," Marley continued. "You two cool with that?"

Target practice continued, unabated. It was as though they didn't hear. Parents steered their children away from the scene, toward safety and home. It was uncomfortable to behold Marley's ineffectual parenting, but I couldn't stop staring. Her gloss was rubbing off before me.

"Hey, guys," I called out. "Listen to your mom."

My words bounced off their gleaming summer bodies like a harmless spray of Nerf gun darts. Marley turned to me, and I felt her focus intensely. Why the look of scorn? She was stubborn and ungrateful, an overextended mother with an inflated sense of self, raising two entitled boys. I almost turned and went inside right then. But I couldn't. What had begun as annoyance had undergone a chemical process in my veins; I was flooded with righteous contempt.

"Serves you right," I said, though Marley was too far to hear.

"Lauren." Someone said my name.

"Who does she think she is, anyway?" I said to no one in particular.

"Lauren." That voice again. Stern and authoritative. Colleen walked toward me, shepherding Violet along before her. Marley stood with her hands folded on top of her head. Tattoos of her boys' names ran along the underside of each arm, elbow to armpit, in ornate cursive ink. Did you love your children more if you needled their names into your skin, did it keep them closer, protect them?

"Let's check on River," Colleen said.

Hunter had moved to stand atop the electrical utility box with his water gun. This put him closer to his target, and the stream of water made contact. The nest swung on its branch. Koda refilled his weapon at the tap. Colleen gently took hold of my arm.

"Coming?" she said.

"No," I said, resisting her pull. I wanted to see what Marley would do next, how she would rein them in, if she even could.

Both boys were on top of the electrical box now, hitting the nest simultaneously. It rocked above their heads like a lethal piñata. They were relentless in their attack; they worked in beautiful tandem.

"Boys." Marley sighed. She moved toward the box, reached up, and placed a hand on Hunter's foot. "Listen to me. You need to stop." She stood almost directly beneath the nest, thirty feet up. Droplets from the boys' guns rained down on her.

"We've almost got it," Koda said. "You'd better move."

"This is the worst idea," Marley said. She looked over to where Colleen and I stood watching at a safe distance. "Move along," she said, and waved her hands to indicate we should go.

I shook my head. No, we weren't going anywhere. The boys were right. The nest was going to come down. Were they more mischievous than other boys, or just curious? If they'd had another mother, would they be so disliked by my neighbours, by me? They were just boys with water guns on a hot summer evening. They drilled into the nest where it connected to the branch.

"Any second now," Colleen said.

"Then what?" I asked.

Colleen shrugged.

The nest fell at an odd angle and a blur of wasps followed it down to where it landed with a soft thud near Marley's feet, a throw cushion tossed from the couch. There was no explosion. It was constructed of paper and built to flex with the wind. The boys whooped in celebration and Marley jumped back, away from the nest, fizzing now that the internal hive had been disrupted.

"Shit," she said, grabbing her ankle. "Get inside," she told her boys. They leapt down from the electrical box, still eyeing the nest, wanting it to do more.

"Go," Marley ordered.

This time they listened. The brothers jogged through the courtyard, spent water guns in hand. I knew that when a wasp stung its target, it also released a chemical message to its colony, ordering them to attack. Wasps flitted around Marley now, spun up and down her long limbs. She started to run for home, with her boys, then stopped and appeared to resist the impulse. She had to go another direction. "Fuckers," she spat, swatting wildly. She ran toward the underground parking garage, trailed by an erratic haze of insects. Out of sight, I heard her shriek—another sting, another several—and the sound echoed through the concrete bunker of parking stalls. Then a metallic crash followed by silence. Had she climbed inside a car? Had she tripped? People stored rusted, flat-tired bikes and other hopeless items where they shouldn't. I could've checked on her, I should have, but I was grateful to her for leading the swarm away from the courtyard, grateful she was gone from view.

"Mama?" I heard River say. Then louder, with a hint of panic, "Mama?"

Maybe later, once the wasps had fully vacated their ruined home, and if the raccoons didn't get to it first, I would tear off a piece to show him. I would point to the branch where it hung, the spot where it fell, and he would know one more thing to look out for in this world. The courtyard was empty, quiet. You could almost convince yourself no one was in trouble, there was no threat of danger.

"Hey, baby," I heard Colleen say. She'd gone to my house, where the front door stood open, and River waited shivering on the threshold. "Your mama's right here." And I was, in an instant. I lifted him into my arms, buried my face in his hot neck, and made the sounds a mother makes to comfort her child, even though he wasn't crying, he was fine.

Shred

If anyone asks, Margot will say she took a wrong turn, strayed from the main hiking trail onto one more popular with mountain bikers. It's approaching dusk. A mild January. Margot is anything but lost.

She tracks the familiar curves and buckles in the path, even jogs a short section because, at sixty-eight, she still can. Overhead, the canopy knocks branches in a way that recalls the fist-bump Margot's grandson, Jacko, now offers with a kiss to accompany "goodbye." The ridiculous farewell, which also serves as a greeting—"knucks," her son, Callum, calls it—is standard among mountain bikers, a kind of punctuation to their rides. They bump fists before donning their full-face helmets and setting off at breakneck speed down the mountain, and then again at the bottom where, mud-spattered and shaking, they squeeze energy gels down their throats in order to do it all over again. They're adult kids who, over the past twenty years, have turned Margot's backyard into a world-class jungle gym for bikes, with elaborate structures drilled into the lower canopy—ramps and shoots, jumps and drops. Callum, thirty-nine years old and living on the east side, still ventures to the North Shore several times a month to "shred."

Margot pulls on her headlamp and directs the beam just off the trail. On her last hike she sourced the logs she'll use tonight. Nothing too big, nothing a bike can't pop over at the last second, especially with the suspension they have these days. Callum is always upgrading, selling his current ride to fund the latest, most aggressive version. There, Margot spies her stash. She casts her beam up and down the trail. Alone. Still, she waits a few beats, closes her eyes, and listens to the night sounds avalanching around her. She's convinced the mountain is communicating with her. She breathes deeply. The smells are so nuanced that an outsider would have difficulty identifying them: licorice fern, mountain heather, bog laurel. But Margot has a nose for this place. She's lived at the base of this cloud-cloaked mountain most of her life, and she appreciates it in ways these adrenaline-junkie mountain bikers do not: down to its very root systems, no, down to its volcanic origins.

Others like her—birders, hikers, and residents whose backyards nudge up against the mountain—are increasingly getting into confrontations with the bikers, swearing matches that spill over onto internet forums: *Nordic walkers need to get a life*; *Doctor required to remove sticks from asses of entitled*

North Shore residents. But Margot doesn't see the point of engaging in these lowbrow squabbles. She'll communicate in the bikers' very tactile language of sticks and stones. Yes, stones. Over the past few weeks, she's been heaving a store of rocks, little by little, closer to the trail. Callum would be appalled. As appalled as Margot had been when, as a teenager, he'd volunteered to help build the trails? Andy insisted she should be glad he wasn't spending his weekends playing Nintendo, was instead hammering together a veritable roller coaster through the trees. Sure, it was about as wholesome an activity as a parent could wish for, but it also placed Callum on the opposing team. Margot tried to convey her displeasure subtly, by ignoring birthday requests for a new pair of knobby tires or logo-enflamed shin pads, but Andy always came through. He'd haul the desired gear from a cupboard after the last presents had been opened, saying something like: "Your mother doesn't want any part in breaking your bones, but I'm okay with it."

Margot opens her eyes. No one coming or going. She gets to work dragging a few logs (substantial branches, really) onto the trail and arranging them side by side. *Entitled North Shore residents*. What do these bully bikers know about anything? How can they possibly share the same level of appreciation as someone who treads lightly, at a pace that allows for contemplation? She and Andy bought their house when no one wanted to live over here, outside the city and up a mountain where weather systems hunker down. How many times did they hike these trails with Callum as a boy? In the early years they carried him in a metal-framed contraption on their backs. Then, as he grew older, they watched him leap ahead, the ascent growing steeper and, miraculously, no more difficult for his young legs. They picnicked on a plateau overlooking Howe Sound, always beside the same weather-stunted pine Callum was fond of monkeying around on, for the wonder of its sturdy though abbreviated limbs. Margot still checks on the tree when she summits. Does Callum remember it?

She hauls another two branches onto the trail and sets them on top of the others. When she's finished, her obstruction is the height of a tall step, not insurmountable, but because of where she's chosen to position it—following a tight bend where it will come as a surprise—a mountain biker should recognize it for what it is: a warning. She stomps over it one way, then back the other. She kicks it, and, satisfied with its placement, its durability, Margot snaps off her headlamp. There's a moon tonight, but even without it, she can hike this trail in her sleep.

CALLUM CALLS THE next morning, Saturday, to ask if Margot will watch Jacko while he goes riding. "Always," Margot says, recalling her mission into the woods last night. Might Callum encounter her booby trap? It will depend on his route. Oh bugger. Might she end up being responsible for her own son's broken wrist? "I look forward to it," she says.

Margot's waiting at the window when they arrive. Jacko waves with both hands while Callum frees him from his car seat. Margot blows kisses. No one loves her like her grandson. She's earned her place at the top—plays on her hands and knees beyond exhaustion, bakes chocolate cakes without occasion.

"G-love!" Jacko shouts. He disappears into the carport and through the door she's left open for them. "G-love?" she hears again at the foot of the stairs.

"Up here," she calls back. She appreciates the nickname Callum christened her with over grandma or nana. G-love and Jacko—they sound good together, a fun-loving duo. She watches as Callum unloads his black beast of a mountain bike from the bed of his truck. "Why do they have to be so ugly?" she'd asked him once. "Burly, Mom, they're burly," was his reply.

Margot feels Jacko's arms clasp her thighs from behind. "Let's play," he says.

"First a walk," Margot says. "Then we'll make cookies."

"I don't want to walk," Jacko whines.

"We might see the fairies this time," Margot says.

"They're always hiding."

"We'll be extra sneaky today." The word that convinces him, of course, is sneaky, and her creeping enactment of what this looks like.

They slip unnoticed past Callum pumping air into his tires, through the wilds of the backyard, and up into the trees.

"I'm tired," Jacko says after only about fifty feet, which, granted, is the steepest part, a root-riddled switchback that connects to a smoother, more traversed trail higher up. Margot agrees to piggyback him the remaining distance, but thankfully, they don't have to go much farther. Up ahead, she sees that her branches have been dismantled and flung to the side. Some early morning "ripper"—Callum has endowed her, whether she likes it or not, with the terminology of this tribe—has destroyed her warning before she can. She's relieved not to see a body in the middle of the trail. She's looking to cause change, not harm.

"Where are they?" Jacko asks.

"Who?" Margot says.

"You said we'd see them, if we sneaked."

"A bird must have warned them. I can't think how else they knew." Jacko's eyes fill with tears. "Oh dear," Margot says, and pulls him into a hug. "You really wanted to catch one of those fairies." Jacko sniffs into her neck. "We'll keep trying," she promises. "Your dad never caught one. But I can tell you're different. You're more in tune with the woods." Margot feels Jacko puff up in her arms, bolstered by the compliment. "I've got a plan for next time," he says.

Callum is gone when they arrive back at the house. Evidence of a smoothie made and consumed covers a stretch of countertop—banana and orange peels, a few stray blueberries, empty yoghurt container, unwashed blender in the sink. Evidence of life, but only silence and mess left behind. The house is too quiet. Margot dials in a pop station on the radio she knows Jacko likes.

"Cookies," he says. "You promised."

"Did I?" Margot says.

"G-love," Jacko scolds, "you know you did."

"I'm so forgetful."

"You aren't."

"Smart boy," she says. "I'm really not."

Margot wipes Callum's mess from the counter. "Is your father a slob at his house too, or just mine?" Jacko doesn't respond, and she realizes her voice has hardened with irritation. She takes a long breath. "He was in a hurry to get out there. He loves that bike, doesn't he?" Jacko nods, yes. "Do you remember where the mixing bowls live?"

Jacko scurries over to the lower cupboards and almost disappears inside. Aside from his pure life force, the way he's always moving, practically bouncing through his days, Margot also loves that he's always talking, that he forces her to talk. Otherwise she can go days without saying a word. She hasn't maintained friendships and now, without Andy, she exists a little outside life. The only thing that reminds her she is, undeniably, alive are her hikes up the mountain, her exploding heart rate and the flood of lactic acid in her muscles as she powers up that first, gnarled slope into the trees. Margot hauls out the flour, sugar, measuring cups and spoons.

"Now, where are those chocolate chips?" she says, pretending not to see Jacko crouched beside the stove with his hands deep in the bag.

• • •

MARGOT AND JACKO are eating warm cookies amid a collection of Callum's old toys when she hears her son return. First the crank of the garden hose as he sprays mud from his bike, then the valve closing and another tap opening, this time the shower in the downstairs bathroom. Callum takes ridiculously long showers, has done since he was a teenager. At first Margot thought he must be doing something adolescent in there, but she later learned, through innocent conversation, that he works out problems under the stream of hot water; it's where he does his best thinking.

Margot's exhausted. Jacko has drained her. She's ready for him to leave. When Callum finally emerges, his face is still bright from his exertions on the mountain. He shoves cookies in his mouth one after the other until he's restored enough calories to finally speak.

"Some funny business going on out there," he says.

"Oh?" Margot says.

"I was talking to these guys. A cable from an old logging operation was strung across one of the trails. At neck height. That could sever someone's spine if he was going fast enough. If he didn't see it."

"Terrible," Margot says, and means it. "That kind of prank isn't funny."

"It's psycho, actually. These are city-sanctioned mountain bike trails."

"Bikers can be a bit territorial, though. Bombing around like they own the place."

"*Bombing* around?"

"Isn't that what you say?"

"I know how you feel, Mom. But this is extreme."

"Don't eat any more cookies," Jacko says. "They're mine."

"If you see anything going on out there, you've got to report it," Callum says.

"Of course I will," Margot says. She thinks of the regulars she passes on her hikes and tries to recall any suspicious backpacks, bulging with more than a water bottle and an extra layer. It could be anyone, someone as unassuming as her, with a grudge, a secret cause. "I'll keep an eye out," she says.

Before they leave, Callum offers Margot knucks, while Jacko places a crumby kiss of unfiltered love right on her lips.

A FEW DAYS LATER, once the stiffness of her previous adventure has subsided, Margot packs a collapsible gardening spade into her oversized hipsack and heads out into a late afternoon spitting with rain. She huffs and pants along the trail toward her rock stash. As she walks, she pulls Callum into her mind's eye. Her only son. Her and Andy's only child. He hasn't offered her so much as a hug since Andy's celebration of life two months ago, hasn't called to check in on her, only to ask her to watch Jacko on his weekends with his son. Would it be so bad if he did break a wrist or an ankle because of her meddling? Then he'd have to sit still long enough to talk to her, maybe even tell her what he's feeling. Or, heaven forbid, listen to how she's feeling. Does a son want to hear these things from his mother, or would he rather not know? Maybe it shouldn't be up to him.

Margot stops in the middle of the trail, places her hands on her hips, and allows her upper body to flop forward. She needs to catch her breath, needs to slow it all down.

"Heads up!" Margot hears from somewhere above her on the single track. A beam of light illuminates bark, sapling, rain. The bike manoeuvres a technical section then turns onto a straightaway and starts racing toward her. "Move!" a male voice shouts. Margot doesn't. Then more aggressively: "Are you deaf?" Light blinds her. The bike's mechanics grind, wet earth rearranges beneath its tires. "Fuck," the biker hisses. Margot smells his personal concoction of deodorant and sweat as he slides past and around her, though just barely, before crashing with his bike a few feet from where she stands. Margot hasn't yet turned on her own headlamp, so she can't make out the biker's face in the gloomy light. His beam leaps around the forest as he works to free himself from beneath his tires.

"What's your deal?" he shouts at her.

"No deal," Margot says.

"Didn't you hear me?"

"I'm out for a walk."

"It's a mountain bike trail. I just about killed you."

The guy crouches beside his bike, checking some component.

Satisfied, he remounts and directs his wheels downhill, away from her.

Margot starts up the trail.

"Hey," he calls after her. "Parking lot's this way."

Margot keeps walking.

"Have it your way," he says.

Her way. What a joke. Is any of this her way? The dead husband, the withdrawn son. The bike judders off, leaving her alone with the mountain. She tucks her hands inside her sleeves and continues briskly along the trail, made springy in parts by the coiled root systems underfoot. As she navigates around fern-festooned boulders and spongy beds of electric-green moss, the confrontation begins to drain through her body and out the soles of her feet. The mountain takes it from her, absorbs the hard minerals of her ire, what might have crystalized, tumour-like, in any other environment. Who's to say the mountain doesn't also have this effect on the bikers? But how can they possibly have time to absorb it, hucking themselves as they do through such splendour?

Finally, Margot comes upon her rocks. Her way, here it is. Her anger may have passed, but her purpose remains unchanged. She shouldn't have to fling herself off a trail into mud and salal every time a biker comes hurtling up behind her, shouting: "Heads up!" No, there isn't room for everyone on the mountain.

Margot shoves, hefts, and arranges. She uses her collapsible spade to lever and roll. Her muscle memory recalls labouring alongside Andy each spring, spreading a truckload of manure on the garden beds, readying them for planting. They worked feverishly, each motivated by the other's thrust, until the beds were heaped with the black gold that would bring forth crops of beans and squash and potatoes. Callum had his own plot where he was allowed to sow his heart's desire, usually peas and tomatoes, until he stopped caring for vegetables or time spent near his parents—maybe just his mother, Margot thinks now. Andy suggested leaving it fallow, in case Callum returned to it post-puberty, but Margot undertook a swift takeover. She filled her son's abandoned bed with raspberry canes, a crop that could never be undone, whether he liked it or not, and continued to expand, sending up canes in far reaches of the yard for years to come, still to this day.

Once the rocks are lined up across the trail, Margot stands back to appraise her work. She's fashioned a wall Jacko would approve of had they been playing a game of fortresses to be scaled by the small figures he carries in his coat pockets.

THE MOB DESCENDS on Margot as she wends her way homeward down a narrow and partially overgrown connector. She hears them before they're upon her: limbs ambushing through underbrush. She's afforded a second to turn and calculate the darkened shapes—it looks like four of them—coming at her before she's thrown to the ground, a knee, or several, landing in her back. Winded. Caught. A chorus of heavy breathing surrounds her but no words. Then, slowly, amid the panting, she hears, *old woman, too small, impossible.* The pressure on her back lessens, then retreats. Margot gasps as her diaphragm steadies and her lungs inflate. She rolls onto her side.

"It's definitely her," says a man's voice. It's the biker she encountered earlier on the trail; she recognizes his rude tone.

"How do you know?" says a woman.

"The shovel."

There's a pause in conversation as the object—Margot's shovel—is passed around and considered.

"It's dirty. She's been busy," says the woman.

"I'm right here," Margot says.

Quiet.

"It's more of a spade," she adds.

"Why do you have a *spade* in the woods?" says the woman.

"I'm digging up ferns for my garden. I know it's frowned upon, which is why I'm out here in the dark." She affects a dithery tone.

"You aren't here for the ferns," a hitherto silent character says. Margot's heart stills. She knows the voice. "Your yard is puking ferns," he says gently.

It's raining a terrific watery applause as the soundtrack to her capture. She's soaked through, her raincoat plastered against her body like a giant Band-Aid.

"Mrs. Doyle, are you all right?" Only one of Callum's friends ever called her that. Atticus.

Although she can't see those full eyelashes blinking disbelief above her, she recognizes his outline, that patient, waiting stance she observed on the sidelines of so many soccer games. Callum's childhood friend had come along camping with them three summers in a row, to Pinantan Lake. He and Callum had learned to fish together, set an alarm, packed food, and pushed off in a rowboat at sunrise. Margot remembers hugging him close when he was perhaps ten, to comfort him in his homesickness on one of those trips. Unlike Callum, who always seemed to stiffen at her touch, Atticus had melted, grateful, into her embrace. Margot recalls her jealousy as she stroked the boy's hair, jealousy that Atticus's mother should get such a prize.

"Does anyone have something warm?" Atticus says. "She's shivering." Margot hadn't realized it, but yes, she's shaking involuntarily, even though she doesn't feel particularly cold.

"I'm okay, Atty," she says, and wonders again now, as she did so many years ago, where she went wrong with Callum. Why was her son, from the time he could walk, running, then riding, always away from her?

"Did you pull that cable across the trail, too?" the woman asks.

"I wouldn't. I'm not sick in the head."

"Kids ride, too. One of your beaver dams could've really messed them up."

So, they've been tracking her, or someone has, taking note of her building projects. Someone alerted them tonight.

"I know where the kids ride," Margot says bitterly. "I know better than any of you."

·

NEITHER CALLUM NOR Atticus, but one of the others in their mountain bike mafia reports her to the police. Margot is put on probation, prevented from walking the trails unaccompanied for a year. Andy's death is pointed to as the reason for Margot's mischief; she isn't coping well, doesn't have many people to talk to. Which is part of it, Margot supposes, but not all. No one considers her complaints about the bikers a valid motive on its own, everyone wants a deeper cause, to unearth something sick and decaying at the root of her. It's annoying. When Callum arrives one day with an agenda, hoping to convince her to sell the house—downsize and move closer to him—she laughs at the absurdity of packing up her life to live nearer a son who appears to want nothing to do with her, other than her babysitting services. She doesn't say this, only that it's too late for her to make those kinds of changes now.

"This place is getting to you, Mom. What you've been up to in the forest, it's not normal." Callum hasn't even removed his coat, still holds his keys in his fist. His right knee jitters. He can't wait to get away from her. "I wonder what Dad would say about your heroics in the woods."

"He'd understand," she says quietly.

Callum leaves behind a pamphlet for a new development in his neighbourhood touting high-end finishes, premium appliance packages, and laughably small patches of shared greenspace. She's glad to see him go, and destroyed by his leaving.

Margot chucks the pamphlet in the recycling bin and shoves her feet into running shoes, pulls on a raincoat. She isn't on house arrest. She wears no GPS tracking device. Who's going to stop her? And, really, what harm in an old woman's pilgrimage up switchbacks, around stumps, over streams, back to the dwarf pine thriving at its stunted rate? Margot brings a hatchet this time (one Andy unbelievably gifted to Callum as a boy), and as she climbs, she's careful to keep her head down and her hood up. But she doesn't encounter another soul—biker or hiker or squirrel. Margot interprets it as a gift from the mountain when she emerges unseen and alone onto the granite slab above the city.

Andy used to sharpen the blade on a grinding stone in his workshop, but now it's dull and bounces off the pine's wintry bark. Still, the grooved handle feels good in Margot's grip, and she doesn't mind that her progress is slow. It might take her more than one trip, but she wants a silvered branch for her mantle. Not a twig, a reasonable limb. Next time Jacko visits he'll ask about it, and then beg for a chance to climb the remarkable little tree, too. He's the perfect size to appreciate its magic. Maybe they'll hike there together, the three of them, and Callum will remember being small, having a mother and father who paused to extract pebbles from his shoes as they climbed, offered sips of water, apple slices. Or not. In which case, at least Margot will have a piece of history, her history. When she can no longer walk the trails, when her memories retreat, finally, into their deepest winter burrows, she'll be the eccentric resident in some assisted-living facility with a branch cradled in her lap or resting on her bedside table. Always close enough to touch.

Fungi

I'm coming on shift, sliding into my Crocs in the staff closet behind the reception desk when my dear Mrs. McTaggart also makes an entrance.

"It's time for Pepper's walk," she snaps to whomever is seated there—Sarah-Jane, Beth-Ellen, Mary-Lou. At Mountain View I work with a disproportionate number of women with hyphenated names; don't ask me who's who.

I slip my phone into my smock pocket. "Good morning, sunshine," I sing, and pop into view.

"Jesus, not her," Mrs. McTaggart snarls. She performs a wobbly about-face and stamps toward the doors, her purple track suit emitting a furious shushing noise as she goes.

"Wait up, buttercup," I say.

"The path's a figure eight. I can't get lost."

It's a game we play. Nearly blind, she knows she must be escorted on walks. Still, she protests. There are others who could accompany her and Pepper, her quaking teacup Yorkie, on the cedar-chipped trails around the home, but frankly, no one wants to, not if they have a choice. Mrs. McTaggart is one sour old pigeon.

"I went on another date last night," I say, hurrying after her. "Don't you want to hear the latest installment? I could use an elder's perspective."

"Elder." She snorts. "That's not what you call us."

"Behind your backs? Well, no."

I don't mind saying that, in general, I dislike my job feeding and cleaning up after old people. I dislike finding them in bed together, am disturbed that shame falls away but desire remains. In hindsight, I should have researched my chosen profession more deeply, but a charismatic speaker on the radio advocating for end-of-life care (why should babies get all the attention?) moved me, and I was pleased to discover the certification was brief. I'd been approaching the job title of career server—which I see now was a better fit for me, managing relationships that last an average of two hours and come with a benefits package of free food and wine—and I panicked. I filled out the application in an afternoon and fudged the volunteer requirement for entry into the program, claimed to have led chair yoga for the brittle and bored at a seniors' centre out of the golden goodness of my heart. I needed a vocation, and I really needed a dental plan. Plus, weren't the Boomers jerking toward the end of life's conveyer belt? There would be no shortage of work. I threw myself into the ethics of elder care. I smiled with audacious empathy not only at actual old people in the street—those avoiding the lethal curb-edge—but also at old-ish ones, those freshly into retirement, who either returned my compassionate gaze with looks of bewilderment or actively looked away.

Let me emphasize that my enthusiasm for the profession peaked *before* I began working as a full-time babysitter for old people, when I was still convinced of the joy and meaning I would inject into their withered lives. What I soon realized was that they no longer cared much for joy or meaning. They'd had all they expected or felt they deserved and wanted only to be left alone, numbing their brains before their private TVs or hunched with their cronies and a full teapot, blathering in a loop about bygone years or gossiping about their neighbours.

No matter. I had steady work and, at last, a mouth guard. I didn't dwell. I kept blood sugar levels stable and learned the names of visiting relatives. I chaperoned dull outings to Stanley Park and alleviated fears that the bus driver on those outings was a terrorist. The trick, I soon realized, was to keep the job interesting, to keep my own brain from going soft.

I gently hip-check Mrs. McTaggart. "I slept with him," I say.

"Good Christ," she says, stopping abruptly, her balance wavering. She has remarkable posture for eighty-eight years old. Still, she's frail and a fall could spell the end. I really shouldn't have bumped her, however lightly.

"It was okay." I shrug.

Pepper rambles off and pees up against a snowberry bush. Somehow it coats both of his quivering hind legs.

"Beau arrives tomorrow," Mrs. McTaggart says. "Pepper and I will be glad not to see your face for twenty-four hours."

"Your grandson Beau? The bomb maker?"

"Watch your mouth," Mrs. McTaggart snaps. "You don't know a damn thing about him."

But I do. She keeps a diary in her bedside drawer. I know Beau's bomb didn't explode, but he'd wanted it to, and for this he spent time in a facility for young offenders down the valley. I even remember hearing about it as a teenager; Beau and I must be close to the same age. From Mrs. McTaggart's journal, I gather he's a recluse of sorts, not to mention the starry centre of her eye.

Mrs. McTaggart veers toward a ditch that is the border between chip trail and brush. I won't let her slip, but admittedly, I wait longer than I should to speak up. I'm fascinated by the lines people cross, the lines people don't even know exist until they're on the other side of them.

"Where are you headed, old gal?"

Mrs. McTaggart stops. "*Amanita muscaria*," she says, staring hard into the brush. I follow her gaze into the tangled mass of ferns and moss. I'm not sure how her milky eyes have spied it, but tucked up next to a boulder, about two metres off the path, is a red-and-white mushroom of the fairy-tale variety. Beyond the boulder looms a ten-foot-high beige wall;

Mountain View is just off the highway. We are, in fact, not meandering along an authentic forest path, but rather plodding a prescribed clover of landscaped dirt surrounded by ineffective sound-barrier fencing. North Shore traffic, mere yards away, is an ever-present tsunami of white noise.

"Those eyes don't work like they used to," I say. "You're seeing things, my dear." I'm not sure why I'm compelled to lie, to make Mrs. McTaggart even more uncertain of her surroundings than she is already.

I take her by the elbow with the intention of guiding her back toward the middle of the path, but she yanks free of my grip and *shush-shushes* away, dragging Pepper by his leash so that he's bouncing across cedar chips. I should keep pace with Mrs. McTaggart, but I decide to give her space. I've pushed her today, though I'm not sure why. I really do appreciate her, in my way. This is where the real rewards of the profession lie, not in masquerading as dignity's accomplice—rinsing false teeth and aiding gnarled fingers with the clasps on vintage strings of pearls. Occasionally, a resident comes along who makes changing linens and talking about the weather worthwhile. What I mean is, one of these husks speaks to you, offers something you didn't expect. My dear Mrs. McTaggart wouldn't be caught dead in pearls, but I know she has a gem in store for me. Through the trees, I catch glimpses of her tacking stiffly along the path. A figure eight; she isn't wrong about that.

For the rest of the day I adjust blankets over chilled laps, read the newspaper aloud, and even pull a piece of gristle from an enthusiastic eater's throat in the dining room. Truth be told, I'm not completely present while all of this is happening. I'm waiting for the phone in my smock pocket to vibrate. I'm *expecting* the phone to vibrate because in a civilized world I would have heard from Jonah by now. Jonah of four dates, who I slept with last night because he wouldn't shut up about how long I'd already made him wait and how he promised to do all manner of pleasurable things to me, promises he promptly forgot once we were wedged into his couch. But it's not a civilized world, is it? And there is no text from Jonah. At thirty-four years old, I'm not new to being ghosted and, therefore, will not stoop to entice him via desperate pleas or jokey nonchalance. The most effective play is to pit silence against silence.

MY SHIFT DOESN'T start until noon the next day, so that night I go for drinks with friends. Not friends, exactly, but colleagues from the restaurant where I last worked, a spare, amber-lit room with clean lines and a view of a city square where many a drug deal goes down under the noses of champagne-sipping, mussel-slurping patrons. My number is still on a group text that goes around about where to meet up for post-work drinks. If anyone thinks it's odd that I continue to join, no one says so to my face.

After two drinks I text Jonah the bar's coordinates in case he wants to resurface. *Out of town*☹, he replies within minutes. Not ghosted, but no mention of where he is, when he might be back, or if he wants to get together upon his return. I confess what I've done to my drinking-mates, and they are both horrified and happy to have something new to talk about. His response time is positive, they say; the emoticon is also promising since it suggests, well, emotion, even if it's false. Their deconstruction is all bullshit I'm willing to entertain in the moment, but in the morning, when I regain consciousness on top of my duvet in a weak puddle of butaned sunlight, there is no way to read the brief correspondence other than pathetic (me) and victorious (him). Once the vomiting subsides, I force myself to jog the trails around the Cleveland Dam as penance for abusing my body and for my general weakness of character.

The days are shortening and the morning light is fleeting and golden, lunging across the trail in organic arabesques. Despite this surrounding glory, I run as if I'm being chased because there's no other way for a woman to run in the woods. Men, even the good ones, are sick of hearing this, but it's true. The Capilano River slides through crevices and canyons on my left and I think of my body being dumped there, my muddy sneakers refusing to sink. My head pounds in time with my footsteps. The trail is set on destroying me, rising and falling at whim. I trip on roots, laced and knotted, and come down on rock. I refuse to assess the damage and stumble on, past the salmon hatchery, its fish ladders built to encourage dying populations to drag out their extinctions a little longer and spawn.

I wouldn't say I don't respect myself, though I'm fairly certain that's what Mrs. McTaggart thinks when I recount episodes from my life. Why do I tell her? Because she has the antidote. I can feel it in the way she looks at me, strips me down to nothing. I trip again. This time, my hands stop my fall. Blessed mud. I wipe my palms on a clump of moss and keep running, limping upward to the top of the dam, where a flood of late-autumn sunlight is my reward. I'm light-headed, jelly-legged. I want to throw myself into the reservoir in baptism. My hip throbs and now I look down to see ripped leggings, flesh scraped and bleeding without commitment. I lean against the railing, chest height to protect against accidents. A raven cruises overhead and lets out a wallop: the sound of a stone dropped from a great height into a deep pool.

THE DOOR TO Mrs. McTaggart's suite is ajar when I pass by, escorting Mr. Yee with a new walker back to his room following lunch. Wet, husky sobs come from inside. I remember that the mythical Beau of Mrs. McTaggart's diary is visiting today and put my hand on Mr. Yee's back to encourage him to speed up, an impossible ask. Before I can take leave of him, he dares to ask for help changing back into his pajamas. I *tsk-tsk*. He pouts and I agree to fetch his slippers. Then I return to the hall and peek into Mrs. McTaggart's sitting room, where Beau, a lumberjack in size and wardrobe, is seated on a footstool weeping into hands like meat hooks. Mrs. McTaggart sits before him, rigid on her loveseat. She stares past Beau, out the window. A hard woman, if ever there was any doubt. I press back against the wall as Beau's sobs lengthen and he tries to regain control of his breath. Pepper's yapping gives me away.

"Just doing my rounds," I say, and knock out a short tune on the doorjamb.

"You," Mrs. McTaggart says, without looking in my direction.

"I *do* work here, and your door *is* open."

"Is this her?" Beau sniffs.

"If you mean one of the people who cares for your grandmother, then yes," I say haughtily, trying to reconcile the knowledge that Mrs. McTaggart has spoken of me to Beau. What has she told him?

"Does Pepper need a walk?" I ask, all business.

"Beau will take him," Mrs. McTaggart says, eyes fixed on the cloudbank outside, "only he's too distraught just now. He wants to leave the land, the land I gave him. I should be bawling, not him."

Beau's head drops back into his hands and the sobbing resumes.

"Well, it's none of my business—"

"No, it's not," Mrs. McTaggart says.

"But shouldn't he be free to leave if he wants?"

"Shut up. You don't know what you're talking about."

I don't bother to feign being hurt. "I'm sure he has his reasons."

From the medieval cursive in Mrs. McTaggart's journal, I know that Beau has been living in a cabin on a wooded lot outside Kamloops for the past ten years, working sporadically for a master timber framer who builds glossy, thick-beamed chalets on a nearby ski hill. As far I can tell, Beau lives alone in the bush. Mrs. McTaggart believes it suits his temperament, calms his destructive impulses, and forces him to think things through. She writes that he would have killed himself—or someone else—ten times over if he lived in the city. Studying the weepy woodsman before me, I'm not convinced.

"I'll take Pepper out—" I start.

"No," Mrs. McTaggart snaps. And now Beau really tries to pull it together. He dries his eyes on a flannel sleeve and stands. It's like watching a mountain form before my eyes—natural forces at work, chaos creating beauty. I don't know where to look; he takes up the whole room. I stare at my feet and feel his eyes assessing my basic flawed humanity, then probing the hideous particulars of it. It's exhilarating and awful. Beau clips the leash to Pepper's collar and ducks out of the room.

For a moment, I'm left alone with Mrs. McTaggart. "Don't you dare," she hisses. "You leave that boy alone."

"What," I say, "could I possibly do?"

Down the hall, the elevator's ping of arrival, then muttering and bumping as a resident greets Beau and Pepper. I move to catch up but stop because there's something Mrs. McTaggart should know: "He's hardly a boy," I say. "A rather fine specimen, in fact." I'm impressed at how unfazed she is, nary a sigh or an eyeroll, not even a snarl. I almost want to take it back, to start again, all gentleness and light. "He seems nice," is all I can say.

IF BEAU IS surprised that I've followed him, he doesn't let on. I admire his unflappability; it strikes me as a challenge. Pepper leads us across the parking lot to the treed loop. Beau's stride is somehow long and slow at the same time, but I pride myself on how quickly I can sync to another's rhythm.

"I know who you are," he says. "It takes a lot to scare me, and frankly, I'm terrified right now."

I stop for a moment, falling behind. "You're kidding, right?" I say to his vault door of a back.

"I don't kid." Pepper scurries over to a pile of debris and releases a weak stream of urine.

"I don't know what stories she's told you, and you're not around that much to gauge her mental capacity, but I'm a health care worker. Health *care*. I'm actually very fond of Mrs. McTaggart, though she misinterprets almost everything I say."

"And then she tells *me* what you say. Why share your sexual escapades with an old woman? We talk a fair bit, even if I don't visit as often as I should. Maybe you didn't know that."

Oh, but I do. Each phone call—date, time, and duration—is recorded in Mrs. McTaggart's diary. Somehow it just never occurred to me that I might be a worthy topic of conversation.

"I don't go into any detail. I'm not explicit. What's so wrong with seeking advice from someone with more life experience?" I'm lying, of course. I *do* go into detail. I *am* explicit. But only because I need to sort through the messy entirety of my situation. I'm as shocked as anyone at the tears blurring my vision.

"You're a narcissist at best, a sociopath at worst," Beau says, unmoved by my display of emotion. He rounds a curve in the path and now his stride gains power; I will have to jog to catch up. But for the moment, I'm stilled. I feel such relief at being called out. I open my mouth and let the meticulously archived bitterness in my body crystalize like a bead of mercury and slide from my tongue. In other words, my mouth hangs wetly open.

"Please," I whisper. "Just, please." And then I run. I run until I'm tripping at his heels. I can smell the aloneness coming off him—different from loneliness. A secluded quarry filled with clear green water at the centre of him. I would dive in, if only he'd let me. I am so close now that I can make out pitted acne scars up one side of his neck, divine constellations. I know what kind of boy he was when he made that bomb: curious, tender, lethal.

"Please, what?" he says, looking down on me as he must look down on everyone. His face is still puffy from crying. His expression isn't angry, nor is it kind.

"Slow down," I say. "I can't catch my breath."

When we emerge from the trees I'm panting and sweating as if I've been running full out. I don't care what I look like. He's already seen me at my worst. He's seen my dark, gilled heart.

An ambulance is parked at the curb, lights flashing without sound. It's a common enough visitor to Mountain View. I can make out paramedics in the lobby manoeuvring a resident toward the entrance. They don't appear to be hurrying, but then they never do, which has always seemed right; it signals levelheadedness, the opposite of panic. Beau must see something too because he scoops Pepper into his arms and vanishes from my side.

I peer in at Mrs. McTaggart before they close the ambulance doors, while Beau tries to convince the paramedics to let him accompany her. Her eyes are pinched shut. She must know I'm watching, but does she also know I feel closer to her than ever? She's done it, as I knew she would all along. Offered me salvation from a hollow, despicable life. I would kiss her feet if she'd let me.

"Be well, my crone," I whisper.

"Excuse me," Beau says, touching my shoulder. I grab the spot in disbelief. The skin beneath my smock throbs.

"Move," he says. This time I shuffle aside and watch as he performs a feat of human origami, folding into the ambulance and positioning himself at Mrs. McTaggart's side.

• • •

I BRING FOOD TO the hospital. I make roasted squash soup and whole-wheat biscuits. I fill Tupperware containers with fresh cut pineapple and kiwi. I leave it at the nurses' station because I'm not family and Beau won't leave Mrs. McTaggart's side to talk to me. The Tupperware is always empty and washed when I return the next day.

I keep coming. I am good at this, persistence in the name of love. It's a trait I honed at a young age, when I fell for the student teacher charged with preparing my Literature 12 class for our final exam. How old was he—maybe twenty-four? I know exactly how old because, while the rest of the class mocked his nerdy jeans, I consumed every detail, both physical—an almost indecipherable lisp, carefully bitten fingernails—and factual—twenty-four with a betrothed named Carmen. I was careful not to appear overly invested in class, neither in the material he taught nor in him. I did not laugh at his jokes (only smiled politely, as though embarrassed for him), nor did I seek him out for supplementary tutelage. I did, however, find out where he and Carmen lived—the top-floor apartment of an old character house, accessible by fire escape—by following him at a safe distance one day after school. I did climb the aforementioned fire escape when I knew them to be out, having waited behind a dumpster one Friday evening and watched them leave dressed for a party. I wasn't setting out to hurt anyone; I was only debilitatingly in love.

Inside, their apartment smelled of spices I couldn't identify then, but that I now know to be turmeric, cumin, and coriander. There were piles of books on every surface, dishes heaped in the sink, and an unmade bed. They were still kids playing at being grownups. I did the dishes. I made the bed. I drew a heart on the mirror using Carmen's red lipstick (so cliché, I know). Then I left the way I'd come, down the fire escape's iron rungs.

No, that's not all. But that's all for now. So, you see, I have a determined streak, barbs that sink in and are hard to shake.

JONAH TEXTS SOMEWHERE in the midst of all this cooking and working and waiting. I don't even bother to reply. I block his number. I don't need distractions when I can feel my life, finally, leaning toward the sun. I run the Cleveland Dam loop each day before work and nod at my fellow runners. I don't fear anyone or anything. I swell like the water churning through the canyon, my heart, my lungs, my mind, inspired, verging on poetic. I review my recipes and hope that today Beau or Mrs. McTaggart will admit me. I will beg their forgiveness. I will apologize for being insensitive, though I do realize I may not get the chance. Reports coming back to Mountain View from the hospital state that Mrs. McTaggart is anemic and disoriented. She's suffering panic attacks and paranoia. I also know she's strong as a bull.

Today, I ride the elevator to Mrs. McTaggart's ward thinking, *Every day is a gift*, and find just that: Beau stooped, feeding coins into a vending machine when I arrive.

"What are you doing?" I say. It comes out more cross than I intend.

"You're back," he says, bending deeply to reach inside the machine. "She said you'd do this."

"I've made sure you don't have to eat this junk."

"Do you really think we'd eat your cooking?"

"Why not?"

Beau shakes his head.

"Like I'd poison it or something?"

"I never said that."

"But that's what you mean."

"Have you tasted any of it yourself?"

"I follow recipes."

"Listen. Maybe you do mean well, but this isn't the time. I'm all she's got." He pauses and I can feel his breath falling around my shoulders like wind off a high plateau. "Are you eating?" he says.

"What? Yes, I'm fine." But it's true; I've lost weight, what with the running and lovesickness. He's observant, my Beau.

"Meet me at the Earls across the street. Seven o'clock. But don't come back here, and no more food."

I MOVE THROUGH MY shift in a dream state. It's Wednesday, the day the onsite hair salon opens its doors. I take residents to and from their appointments and compliment their freshly set permanents. I settle a dispute at the card table with unusual patience. I encourage stragglers, those staring blankly at walls and tabletops, to join the crowd gathering in the chapel for a piano recital performed by someone's prodigious grandchild. I am beneficent and detached. If only I could be this way every day.

On my lunch break I let myself into Mrs. McTaggart's suite. Housekeeping has tidied and left the window open to encourage airflow. I take her journal from her bedside drawer and flip to the last entry. It was written the night I went out and got drunk, the night before Beau arrived.

> If you're reading this, I can add snoop to your list of improprieties. I've told Beau everything. You have one week to hand in your resignation, or I will make the fuss you know I'm capable of.

I blink back tears. I laugh. That's my girl. How I would love to have known her as a young woman. I think we would have been friends. I believe I would have confided in her, even then. She might have saved me from myself. *Don't you dare go to his house again*, she might have said. *Leave him alone; he's not worth it.* Maybe I would have listened. As it was, though, I had no one. I had an imbalanced teenage mind, a serious case of infatuation. Of course I went again.

I arrive early at the restaurant. Beau hasn't made a reservation, so I sit at the bar and wait. I order a cocktail, then think better of it. I don't want to appear to have vices, especially when Beau appears so monkish and pure. I down the cocktail, push the empty glass toward the bartender along with a twenty. I fold my hands in my lap and concentrate on the fish in the aquarium behind the bar, the soft Os of their mouths bumping against the glass.

Beau's hand on my shoulder. "There's a table."

"Yes!" I practically leap off the barstool. Too eager. Too alive. I don't care. This is exactly what I want him to see. I follow him through the room to a table with two chairs and a great expanse of dark wood between place settings, too great for intimacy of any kind. But I'll take what I can get.

"We've talked to management," Beau starts. "We're pushing to have you fired, or at the very least moved to a different care facility."

"Fired?"

"For misconduct."

I imagine my hideous red wine–stained teeth without my biannual dental hygiene appointments.

"We haven't engaged a lawyer. Yet."

The distance across the table is so vast, I'm not sure my words will reach him. I open and close my mouth. I rise from the table and sit back down.

"I've been waiting for this," I say. "Not this, exactly, but something like it. It's the only thing that works for me. I need to be found out, turned in, told off. It's the only way I can change."

Beau doesn't respond, just looks down at the water glass

encased in his giant hands. "That sort of makes sense," he says finally. "But it doesn't fix anything."

"She doesn't believe it, but I hold your grandmother in very high esteem."

"It's anxiety, mostly. The symptoms. Heightened by your insensitivity. Your, from what I'm told, *unceasing* insensitivity."

"That's a tad extreme."

"She's nearly ninety. I think you must forget who you're dealing with sometimes."

We haven't ordered food. No one has even come to our table. Maybe it was never Beau's intention to dine with me, only to meet in a public place for safety, with witnesses. It crushes me a little.

"What did you want the bomb to do?" I ask. "I mean, if it had exploded, what were you trying to say?"

Beau sighs. "I didn't really want to hurt anyone. Just wake them up. Make them realize they were going to die. At some point. Everyone went around acting like it would never happen to them. But it was all I thought about."

Which was also the verdict about me, in the end. A young girl's preoccupation gone haywire, mutated. Though at first it wasn't viewed that way. For a while I was considered a real threat.

The second time I visited, I found their bedroom window open and climbed in after midnight, while they slept. Dirty laundry strewn on the floor of their bedroom, the way it was in my own. The vulnerability of his face at rest, almost babyish, disgusted me slightly. I almost aborted my mission. Carmen's hair was flung across her face, and she snored loudly. I went into the living room and saw a stack of marking on the coffee table next to an empty Dairy Queen cup. I rifled through the papers for my essay and found it slashed with a *C-*. I was hurt that my attempt to write something comprehensible, injected with sudden stabs of beauty, something that would set me apart, hadn't been recognized. The paper wasn't why I'd come, though. I was no longer fueled by love. Quite the opposite.

Earlier that same day I'd raised my hand in class, something I never did. I'd tried to contribute to the discussion. There were others with questions and juvenile epiphanies, which he acknowledged or addressed, taking care to respond fully, but he actively ignored me. I didn't imagine it. My classmates snorted and murmured when the bell rang and he began gathering his things, my hand still raised. I couldn't bring it down. I was too proud, too invested. I sat like that until everyone left. Maybe he suspected me of the first break-in. Maybe it was punishment for my perceived sour attitude up to that point. Neither, though, was a solid enough reason to ignore me so blatantly. I remained alone in that sun-torched classroom, my hand raised insistently, stubbornly, my brain awash with rage, a feeling that had begun to increasingly overwhelm me. It left me breathless to consider my potential in these moments, what I might be capable of accomplishing when powered by such internal force. It was this force that carried me back to his apartment that second time.

I placed my essay back in the stack, in alphabetical order by last name. I looked around for some way to reciprocate for the way he'd treated me in class earlier that day. Then I saw the satchel he shouldered lovingly into class like a dumb fifth limb. Inside, I found his prized volume—his great-grandfather's, I believe—of *The Complete Works of William Shakespeare*. I streamed my thumb across the heirloom's gilded pages and began tearing them out one by one. I walked circles around the room, letting them fall. Gradually, I forgot my anger, so mesmerized was I by the carpet of text I was creating. It felt like great art, in a way.

"Are you hungry?" Beau asks. His voice arrives across the mahogany divide as though via two-way radio at sea: garbled, doomed. I can't remember how I landed here. Not at Earls, but here, in life. It seems that while others have been taking practical steps toward reasonable goals, I've been walking with my feet turned inward, misstepping.

"I hoped you and I..." I say. "There might be something."

"I don't think I gave you that impression."

"You didn't. Like I said, I hoped."

"Hope is good, I guess."

"I care for her, you know, even if she is a thief, which may or may not surprise you." I try to hold the stormy centres of his eyes in my gaze and feel myself going cross-eyed. "She's not the only one. They all steal from one another. It's funny, actually. They think no one notices."

"I don't see it, to be honest. My grandmother has scruples."

"Oh, well, they all do, but those fall away. There's a sloughing off that happens—inhibitions, good sense, moral codes."

"I believe that's dementia. She doesn't have dementia."

"It's fascinating, you know? Our desire to possess *things*. What good do they do us in the long run?"

"What sorts of things are we talking about?"

Truthfully, I've never witnessed Mrs. McTaggart steal anything. Others, yes, but not her. Telling lies is my juvenile attempt to self-soothe.

"Why has no one come to our table? The service here is terrible." I can feel it rising again, that rage that separates me from the rest of humanity. I'm better on my own. My shoulders fall, and I almost wet myself in gratitude. He's not so good looking. He's either greedy and bullish in bed, full of apology afterward, or self-conscious and impotent, neither of which I have the patience for. Good riddance.

"I could eat pasta, heaps of pasta," I say. Beau doesn't respond. He's mixing powders in his mind, measuring potential outcomes. "I got into this for the right reasons," I continue. "Midwife on the other end of life is how I imagined it."

"It's not what you expected, sure. But that's not my grandmother's fault. That's no reason to take it out on her."

"I misread her. I thought she was tougher. For that, I'm sorry. For the rest, I can't say that I am."

As I wasn't sorry about *The Complete Works of William Shakespeare*. It might have been a family heirloom, but it was just a *thing*. The way he behaved I might as well have destroyed the only known copy of the master's work. It was Carmen, the fiancée, who found me, or, more precisely, I found her. The creaking floorboards caused my eyes to lift, though without pause in my blasphemy. She appeared more disgruntled than startled or afraid, and I thought, that's how I want to react in the face of uncertainty, even danger: annoyed. Her arms were folded across her breasts and her underwear was nothing special. I'd almost finished with the pages—comedies, tragedies, histories. The book's spine was a gutted column of loose threads. It was he who finally entered the room shrieking and swatting at me with a broom. A broom!

"Mr. B!" I shouted. "It's me, Samantha Jervis from Lit 12, wake up!"

"I am awake, you little bitch," he said. "You're my living nightmare."

Finally, a waiter wafts within earshot.

"I'll have the ravioli con fungi," I say, "lots and lots of fungi. And a glass of white wine." The waiter nods. "For you?" he says to Beau.

"Ditto. No wine."

We wait for our food in amiable, and, at least for me, arousing, silence. It's so easy to be with this man and say nothing. It's heaven to sit in his shade. He's probably a genius. Oh, dammit. I think I do love him.

"Do you ever feel like you're only half alive? Like you're skating over the surface of your finite days without ever allowing yourself to think or love too deeply?" I spit the words like a mouthful of water into his face.

"I do," he says.

We're quiet again until the food arrives.

After Mrs. McTaggart had drawn my attention to the *Amanita muscaria* on our walk that day, the sighting I had, inexplicably even to myself, denied, I'd returned at the end of my shift to destroy it. I leapt over the ditch and into a clump of ferns. Even up close, the mushroom looked fake, like a garden gnome's stone accompaniment, but when my clog came down on its red hood, the body collapsed easily, fleshily, beneath my sole. I ground it into the earth, into what I knew was only a temporary death.

"Mushrooms are fingers from the underworld," I say, slurping at morels, chanterelles, porcinis, all bathed in an ungodly rich cream sauce I will have to run like a demon from her exorcist to burn off. Across the table, which I now see as a perilous though not impassable bridge to be crossed, Beau nods, unable to speak because his mouth is full.

The Day the Children Left

The children woke coughing. Smoke hung above their beds, so they dropped beneath it, dressed lying down. In neighbouring rooms their parents stirred, but none could shake their anchored dreams in time to stop the children leaving. The older ones collected babies from cribs or drew them from their sleeping mothers' breasts. They'd already waited too long. The world was burning and all their mothers could manage to do was sweep drifts of ash from the front steps; their fathers shushed them, spun the radio static for answers. The children had answers. They coughed into their sleeves as they walked away from their homes, down moonscaped boulevards, as their parents should have done months ago.

WHEN THE PARENTS WOKE, they didn't remember their children. They felt an absence, but of what they couldn't say. Even the empty beds, the mothers' leaking breasts, the toys underfoot didn't jog their memories. Still, a mysterious urgency fluttered in their chests, sent them hurrying room to room. A picture book left open, a smashed piggy bank in the corner. The longer they stared at these things, the less they understood them. So they began to look away. They had more time to sweep. They feared the fires less because they were only afraid for themselves. One mother finally drank the good tequila; her resulting headache obliterated any hope of remembering. Her husband agreed it was peaceful in a way it hadn't been in years.

THE CHILDREN WALKED and walked until they reached the river. No longer the mighty salmon spawning grounds of history books, its waters ran low and iridescent. The children abandoned the strollers on the trash-choked banks. The oldest, a freckled bolt of a girl, did a head count, then instructed the others to make a human chain through the sludge and ferry the youngest across in their arms. She was vigilant, counted again on the other side. Filthy and shaking, they collapsed beneath a maple's bare limbs and ate stale crackers and jellybeans. The babies cried for milk, but they would soon forget. No one argued. There were gulps of sadness. The girl stripped to her underclothes, draped her mucky jeans over a rock to dry. Then she returned to the river's edge, looked back in the direction they'd come. No one moved. She coughed once and spat in the slimy shallows. Then she picked up a rock, chucked it in. Gradually, the others joined her and did the same. The river boiled with stones and its bank was noisy with the grunts of the children hurling them. Soon, though, the babies began to wail. They wailed to feel something akin to fresh air on their faces—an absence of smoke, anyway. The children's hands fell back to their sides, and no one coughed as they had before.

WHERE IS IT? *What am I looking for?* the parents wondered as they climbed upstairs, downstairs, forgetting to eat, bathe, sleep. They bumped into one another, bounced off one another, paid more attention to the animals. Eventually, the dogs walked away from their stroking hands. The smoke grew so thick it shuttered the sun. No one knew it yet (yes, the dogs did), but the planet was dead. They felt it, though, a quickening like the last sluice of bathwater down the drain. It was someone's fault, but whose? Those people in the neighbouring town, and the towns to the north, south, east, and west. The parents were furious, and their rage quashed the uneasiness they'd felt since the children left. One father almost remembered. He sat on the sofa nuzzling the soft underside of his forearm, compelled, even, to caress his own flesh.

"What are you doing?" his wife asked.

"Here," he said, offering his arm. "What does this remind you of?"

THE DAYS WERE diabolically hot, but not toxic as at home. With no one to tell them otherwise, the children stayed up too late. The babies rolled and crawled about the tinder forest floor while their siblings scavenged withered berries and parched clover or hung like cheetahs in the crumbling arbutus trees. Each breath was a feast for their small lungs. Within hours, it seemed, they grew thinner, taller, adapting to their new environment. One night, a vulture hauled a baby three feet off the ground before the others could beat it away. After that, they grew serious, divided into groups and fashioned surprisingly sound shelters. They rationed what food they'd brought and hunted for more. The forest was sick, yes, but there were still a few rodents left to be skewered. The freckled girl offered to catch bottom-feeders, but the others worried she might sneak off, scurry back the way they'd come. "Why would I go back?" she said. No one knew why—the blisters that had erupted on their skin after crossing the river were only just beginning to heal. They knew only that she couldn't. She was the first who'd thought to rock the babies, the first to string their names into a lullaby that carried them to sleep.

THE PARENTS GREW ILL. Their ribs began to crack from the coughing. Their animals, the all-knowing dogs, died. They wheelbarrowed the creatures' bodies to a canyon the fire had yet to jump, dumped them in, and stumbled blindly back to their homes. Inside, they sealed the doors and windows with their children's bedding and lay curled like abandoned seashells on the floor. Sometimes they felt quick footsteps vibrating through the boards beneath them and opened their eyes, expecting to see what? They only saw one another. Maybe they were already dead. If not already, then soon.

THE GIRL WORKED all day to haul a sluggish sturgeon from the river muck with her bare hands. Near dusk, exhausted and sore, she finally encircled its ancient body of watery memories with her arms. She felt its old-world currents in her blood, and her thirst for the river of a hundred years ago was bottomless and bygone. Rank with slow death, the sturgeon didn't protest its capture; it only looked so mournful that she was forced to let it go.

She suggested to the others it was time to move on; they could once again taste smoke. Particulate grated the undersides of their eyelids. The children gathered cross-legged on the bank, skimming their hands over raspy clumps of dead moss. The girl was tall and strong the way girls often are before boys outgrow them, but even the tallest boy lowered his gaze. The children watched as their dinner, the sturgeon, burrowed into the earth's sour embrace and forgave her. They understood she was their leader. They made a circle around her and wiped the mud and stench from her limbs with the cuffs of their sleeves. She shivered, hugged a baby close, and craved the heat of her mother's thighs when she used to slide her cold feet between them.

ONE NIGHT, WHILE the parents slept, it rained enough to extinguish the fires, which is to say biblically, unnaturally. The ash turned to mud and rose to their front doors, spilled through the cracks. They woke trying to sweep it away from their sides, creating sludgy angels on the floor around them. They crawled upstairs to escape it. They were almost happy for the change, a roar that wasn't flames. They looked in the direction of the fires, where they'd burned for so long. With the smoke now cleared they saw houses like their own, windows imploding as the waters rose. People were climbing out onto their roofs to await rescuers who would never arrive. One woman waved.

THE RIVER SURGED; its banks disappeared. The children had not left in time. They climbed trees until they looked out over the forest canopy, which, the girl realized, was really just a collection of skyward-reaching sticks. Crawling among them, they were last gasps of green. Or were they locusts? They were both, she decided, and almost fainted at this truth. There was nothing she could do, nothing any of them could do. She wove her way through the branches, kissing the other children's heads as her father had done the last time it snowed, the same year she learned to walk. Even with the fires extinguished, a hot wind continued to blow. The trees swayed. Soon their brittle roots would disengage from the earth, and, at last, they would all fall down. For now, though, the bigger children held the babies tightly, fearful of dropping them. When the babies opened their mouths to cry, they filled with bitter rain. There was a loud crack upstream, followed by groans and claps. A house rounded a bend in the river, its walls unfolding as it tore past on the muddy current. They recognized the house. The bloated remains of a dog sailed past next. They thought they recognized the dog, too.

THE PARENTS CLUNG to what they could. They looked around for someone to blame. Those who'd managed to climb into boats rammed their oars into passing ones, trying to capsize them. They couldn't yell (smoke had destroyed their voices), but they stretched their mouths around screams. The flood fed all of them—the people from the towns to the north, south, east, and west—into the river and swept them downstream. They were glad to be leaving and frightened to die. In the boats their laps felt light when they should have been heavy. One mother almost remembered. She squeezed her hands between her thighs.

THE RAIN EASED and the sky became less dull. "Look," one of the small ones called out, "over there." In the canopy, in the distance, more children. Where had they come from? To whom did they belong? Below, on the swollen river, two boats rounded the bend. "Mom!" the girl shouted. The boats were at odds, trying to upend each other. "Mom!" the children called in crow-like chorus. It was all of their mothers. It was none of them. The warring adults were too preoccupied to look up. Or they didn't hear over the rushing water. The adults had forgotten who would inherit the earth. Or they no longer cared.

THE GIRL SLIPPED on a branch and caught herself. Even at a distance, she felt the group of unknown kids watching. Then something pelted her shoulder: a sun-parched pinecone. Next, a shower of them, a siege. There was laughter from one side, cries from the other. The girl thought she recognized one of them, a boy close in age she'd often seen riding a red bike past her home.

Beneath them, the waters had begun to recede and soggy islands appeared like prized sand dollars. On both sides, the babies were bawling and the smaller children were scared. The girl knew she had to climb down and face whatever awaited. What would they eat? Where would they sleep? She longed to share these worries with someone else. After all, she was only thirteen.

She lowered herself down a branch, then another, another, until finally she dropped to the ground. Immediately, she sank to her knees in mud. She withdrew one foot, but the other sank deeper. Panic made her lightheaded; the earth was about to swallow her whole. *At least I'll be done worrying*, she thought, *at least I'll sleep.* The mud rose almost to her hips.

Something hard knocked her on the head then, and she thought the rival children had come to finish her off, but it was only the boy, crouched on a nearby rock, holding an oar out toward her. For a heartbeat the girl considered giving in to her exhaustion, but then cheers started up in branches overhead. A riotous chorus of whoops and bellows and shouts. Her wayward family urging her on.

The Intruder

The woman let herself into the kitchen just before seven on Tuesday morning. I thought it was Rory coming home from her boyfriend's since Satan didn't bark. I'd been up most of the night worrying about her spending so much time in a house where four teenage boys paid the rent. They weren't, in fact, teenagers anymore, but barely. And did that make it any better? Rory was seventeen.

I hadn't locked the door after taking Satan out that morning. Like I said, I was expecting Rory; the brisk opening and closing of the door was done with a proprietary hand. I was on the couch scrolling through filtered realities on Instagram. I'd joined solely to follow Rory, which she knew, just as I knew she had another, private account where she posted truer photos of her life. My handle was @satan_sleeps and my gallery exclusively chronicled the life of my geriatric black lab, sometimes ambling down a wooded path, often in my bed, tolerant of the coffee and newspaper I set on a tray beside him for effect. I wanted nothing more than a like from Rory and my sister in Calgary.

"Ror, come here," I said, hoping my grown girl would curl up beside me on the couch, and I would be able to ignore the smell of sex on her skin and weed in her hair. (She claimed not to smoke on school nights but couldn't prevent others from doing so.) Rory didn't come, she didn't even groan at my request, which was what prompted me to stand.

It wasn't Rory in the kitchen.

The woman kept her hand on the doorknob, twisting it slowly back and forth. She was barefoot and wore what looked like the underpinnings of a Victorian dress—a crinoline, I guess—and a loose hoodie. Her head was shaved and it suited her, in the same way it did the American girl who'd survived a high-school shooting and was now an activist for gun control in the US, though my intruder was at least ten years older than that girl.

"I don't know you," I said, "so it's time for you to leave."

"I live on First Ave.," she said. "Not far from here, but I can't go back. It's not safe."

"Get out," I said, the uncharitable words popping from my mouth like hot rocks from a fire. "Get. Out."

She opened the door and stepped outside, onto the welcome mat. Looking down at her bare feet she said, "I need help," as if she were embarrassed, for me, at having to state the obvious.

"I could call the police," I said, letting the screen door slap shut between us.

"Please. Don't."

I knew the area of First Ave. she was referring to, a relatively new block of transitional housing, a ten-minute walk from my door. Recently, I'd overheard a neighbour complaining about the influx of destitute souls trawling our walkways for strollers and poorly secured bikes. I didn't ask how he knew, but he said the VPD had visited that address seven hundred times already this year.

"They might help," I said, though clearly the woman knew better than I what the police could or couldn't do for her.

"They'll dump me in psych. I can't go back there."

My mind seized upon a time when I probably should have gone to psych, after Rory was born and I wanted only to fall asleep and never wake up. But her cries were the toothpicks that held my eyelids open. I never slept, and while awake I experienced graphic, unannounced visions of the myriad ways I might harm my new baby: pushing her stroller out into traffic, spilling hot coffee on her delicate skin, removing my hand from beneath her floppy head in the bath. I can't even utter my darkest imaginings now, as I couldn't utter them then to get the help I needed. I was convinced if I did, Rory and I would be separated, so I kept my fears to myself.

I heard kitchen stirrings on the other side of the wall in the neighbouring townhome. It made me feel safer, less alone. It softened and emboldened me.

"What were you looking for in my kitchen? What made you think to let yourself in?"

"I wasn't thinking. I just needed a place to go." She paused, clarified, "*Need* a place to go."

The woman lifted one foot and placed it against her calf muscle, as a dancer might. She stood like that, hands tucked in the front pouch of her hoodie, balancing in the walkway outside my home. I could see she might be hiding something in her sweatshirt, something stolen, maybe, or something growing, like a baby.

"Do you want a banana?"

"Coffee would be great."

"Coffee."

She placed her foot back on the ground and raised the opposite one into the same position. I realized she might be doing it to keep from feeling the cold. I pointed to my gardening clogs. "Put those on, if you want," I said, and closed the door. The sound of the deadlock clicking into place was at once practical and over-reactive. I filled the stovetop espresso maker with water, then inserted the little metal bucket of grounds.

The woman wasn't on drugs that I could tell. She was actually quite poised. My neighbour exited her house and passed the woman on our shared path. I heard a tight exchange of good mornings. On the boulevard, the red maple shook free its valentine-bright leaves. The coffee steamed and sputtered. I released the deadbolt and opened the door. "Milk? Sugar?"

"Do you have soy milk?" she said.

"No."

"Black, then. Please."

Satan clopped into the kitchen and sat on my feet while I poured the coffee.

"Some guard dog," I said, stroking his sleek skull. Outside, the wind began gusting. I delivered the woman's mug and invited her to sit in one of the Adirondack chairs on the communal deck.

"I'd prefer to go inside," she said. All around us autumn leaves spun upward like flocks of small, panicked birds.

"I know," I said. "But I think you can understand why I might not be comfortable with that."

"Not really," she said, sitting and wedging her crinoline between her thighs. "Just imagine me outfitted in GAP, and with more hair."

I did. I imagined her in the uniform of the day: skinny jeans, ankle boots, fashionably shapeless overcoat. Would I take her in then? I had the space, of course, especially now that Rory only came home to shower and change. Recently, the intrusive thoughts had returned, only now they didn't feature what damages I might inflict on my daughter, rather what the world might do to her. I imagined her being pulled from a car wreck or trapped in a classroom during a school shooting. Even though I had met all four boys in the house where she mostly lived, and they seemed kind, if directionless, I imagined them raping her. It was ludicrous, and it wasn't. I texted Rory for her whereabouts when these scenarios began rampaging through my head.

"I have a pair of fleece leggings that might fit you," I said, noting that the woman was wearing my clogs. She shrugged.

"Why isn't it safe," I asked, "for you to go home?"

"Would it change anything if I told you?" she said, wrapping her hands tightly around my mug. "Like, could we go inside?"

I looked at my phone. Rory should have been home by now. It was a school day. She always came home before her first class. Apparently, the bathroom at the boys' house was vile. I texted: *You're late.* The woman set the empty mug at her feet. I saw goosebumps stippling her calves. I saw no evidence of bodily harm, but I also knew that meant nothing. She stood and pulled a bunch of bananas from beneath her hoodie. The bulge I'd thought might be a baby deflated.

"I don't even like bananas," she said. Rory didn't either, yet I continued to buy them, for the potassium, a quick fix for hunger.

I saw Rory arguing with a jealous boyfriend, struck dead in a crosswalk, slumped unconscious in a bush. My chest tightened and I tried to draw a deep breath. As a young mother, I'd briefly believed I was possessed, my unbidden, demonic imaginings evidence of another spirit moving through me. I wondered sometimes, still.

A car pulled up and Rory emerged, coughing. The wind delivered the skunky fragrance to where the woman and I stood.

"Mom, god," Rory said, keeping her head lowered as she strode toward us down the walk, ankle boots clicking.

"You can't go to school like this," I said.

"I'm fine," Rory said. "I just need to eat something." She flicked the doorknob and reached inside to offer Satan her hand. The woman slid out of my gardening clogs and pulled her hood up over her head. In fact, the crinoline and sweatshirt looked like a costume a dancer might really wear.

"Do I know you?" Rory said.

"We're neighbours," the woman said.

"Okay," Rory said. Then to me: "Tell me you got groceries. And, no, I don't want a banana." The cluster remained on the chair where the woman had left them, a bright rebuke.

"There's plenty of food," I said, feeling both guilty for possessing such abundance and irritable with my daughter for not knowing abundance if it fell on her head.

"You hungry?" my daughter asked the woman.

"I'm more than that," she said.

Rory nodded as if she knew what that meant, as if she, too, had needs beyond what I could provide for.

"We're going to talk about this," I said, waving my hand at Rory, her overall state, the makeup smudges around her eyes, her eyes in general. "Go shower." She shook her head as if she couldn't believe what I was saying. It quite enraged me, the dismissal implied in that headshake.

"You're too trusting," I spat. "You're naive."

Rory looked at me as if I'd just flipped a sublimely set table at a dinner party: incredulous, appalled.

"And you're paranoid," she said. "You see danger everywhere. You *want* to see it."

"I *want* to see you trampled in a nightclub? I enjoy visions of you being abducted off a dark sidewalk into a van—"

"Mom."

"What?"

"Enough."

Rory was right; my voice was tightening, inching toward hysteria. Certainly part of me hoped the world *would* always appear a kinder place to her eyes than it did to mine, but the other part of me wanted her to sniff its sour underbelly so that she would always recognize the smell, know when to back away.

At that moment, though, standing outside the threshold of our home, there was no threat of danger that even I could claim to detect. I'd felt the woman's curiosity and, possibly, her judgment as she stood watching my exchange with Rory, stoned out of her tree on a school morning. I wanted to ask what she was thinking. I needed her advice. *Rory* needed her advice. I could only ever share with her the hazards I'd encountered on my rockslide into adulthood. But if this woman would share hers, also, maybe Rory would be better prepared; maybe she'd make better choices than either of us had. Only later, recounting the story to my sister, was I finally able to grasp the reality of the situation: the wind was cold, the woman's skirt a mesh sieve, and I was just another person content to give her nothing and, incredibly, expect something in return.

Hyacinth

Today, the first Saturday in February, a slushy rain falls as Cameron Hornby feeds his coin into the locked row of carts. He yanks one free and steers it awkwardly—for there is no other way to manoeuvre the supersize gurneys—across the parking lot toward the store's entrance spilling forth Valentine's decorations and potted hyacinths in various stages of bloom. The strong floral scent makes him ache for spring, which he assumes is the point, and he puts one in his cart on a whim. In general, he's a careful shopper, wary of hyped deals and attractive displays, but surely everyone strays on occasion.

"It's easy to convince yourself you need a dozen cans of baked beans," he'd said to his favourite cashier, Jane, when he first started going through her till several months ago. "But unless you're stockpiling for Armageddon, you probably don't."

"True," she'd said, scanning his bale of toilet paper, a perfect example of a staple that *should* be bought in bulk, but Cameron held back, cognizant that talking about toilet paper and everything it implied might be crass.

Jane zapped his economy-size tray of chicken breasts next.

"Actually, you got me," Cameron said, raising his hands in surrender. "I'm a survivalist."

"This will be a real treat in your bunker," Jane said, hauling through his wife Meg's flat of grapefruit-flavoured bubbly water.

"Practically champagne," Cameron said, thrilled with the playful note they'd struck.

"How would you like to pay for your provisions?"

"Indeed, my comestibles," he said. "My rations for the dark days ahead."

"Yes," Jane said. "Those."

Cameron was confused until he realized she was asking him to produce a credit card and move on. Of course. They couldn't very well stand there chatting all day.

Today, as always, he's come prepared with a few anecdotes about whatever happens to be in his cart, or in the news, so that he and Jane can make the most of their brief time together. His hyacinth is a perfect place to start. "How frivolous of you," he imagines Jane saying with a hint of mockery, and he will take a certain pleasure in knowing the shopper behind him is observing their exchange.

Inside Buy-It, Cameron looks for Jane's messy bauble of

black hair along the row of checkout counters. There she is, in her red apron, in lane number ten. He hopes she isn't on break when he's finished shopping. He has, on occasion, loitered in the aisles, awaiting her return before getting in line to pay.

IT'S STUPID, JANE knows, but she's asked her manager to permanently switch her from Saturday to Sunday mornings. Maybe she didn't sound desperate enough because her schedule remains fixed.

Cameron Hornby is nobody, harmless, but something about how much he cares, his premeditated jokes, his stunning recall of the little she's revealed about herself—accidently, before she realized he was taking note—makes her uneasy. She's begun to anticipate, if not dread, her Saturday morning encounter with him. Just last night her subconscious had conjured his melon-bald head while she sipped a pint with friends. The pub door had swung open and she saw him as she would the following morning, holding up shoppers inside the store entrance while he cast about trying to ascertain her whereabouts. It rattled and perturbed her. But why? He's just a regular, one of many. And yet this morning in the shower with Gabe, his fingers moving like a liquid current inside her, Cameron Hornby's groomed fingernails selecting a credit card from his wallet had slipped into her mind, interrupting her pleasure; she'd nearly concussed herself twisting away from her boyfriend's touch.

Jane knows her discomfort around Cameron Hornby is either irrational or intuitive, and it strikes her as deeply unfair that she can't identify which.

"Is he pervy?" Gabe asks when she admits what spooked her in the shower. "Is that what you're picking up on?"

"No. I don't know. He's too eager. Too familiar."

"Could be lonely."

"That's *my* problem?"

"It's kind of, like, society's problem?"

Jane wants to roll her eyes at his goodness, his naïveté. A married man should not be looking to a cashier for comfort in this failing world. She doesn't know what he should be doing instead, but it definitely shouldn't involve her. Jane's legs span Gabe's galley kitchen like a bridge. She watches as he prepares poached eggs and tosses smoothie ingredients into the blender, occasionally ducking beneath her knees to get a plate or a spoon from the other side. It is, in fact, her galley kitchen now, too, only it doesn't feel like it yet. Her boxed-up belongings, which are surprisingly few, are still stacked in the narrow entranceway. She and Gabe had been seeing each other for five months when his roommate left; it just made sense to move in. Jane wanted to be with Gabe, but even more so she wanted to escape her current living situation, a house of women where petty hostilities were brewing. It had been utopic for a while, with nights of ukulele music and talk of a road trip to California in a rented motor home, but they were all four recent art school graduates, and the pressures of the artless world were fast creeping in. Jane had been the first to fold and apply for a job at Buy-It. The others were appalled, still high on the fumes of student loans and credit.

"A cashier?" Arwen, the unofficial head of the household said. "Mindless work. Soulless." Truthfully, Arwen was the main reason Jane had to leave. Her opinions were so strong that Jane's critical brain had begun to atrophy; she couldn't gauge how she felt on a particular topic until Arwen held forth.

Jane was fairly certain she felt the opposite about her job at Buy-It, even though she couldn't, at the time, articulate why. After only a week at Gabe's, though, a week of relearning how to think for herself, she understood she felt relieved to know a massive corporation was behind her paycheque; she was anchored to an iceberg of wealth, a small portion of which she was entitled to for merely tapping in codes. She was not working in an upstart café where she might be admonished for putting a slice of lemon in her water, because had she seen the price of lemons lately? She was not fulfilling a pathetic six-week contract, working on spreadsheets for a non-profit arts organization out of a mildewed basement apartment, where she was asked at the end of her day to make a liquor run for her supervisor, if such a title could be bestowed on a chain-smoking fifty-something-year-old who spent the day entering vacation getaway contests online. No, at Buy-It the lighting was fierce, the rules were clear, and the paycheque would keep coming as long as she wanted it to. And maybe the mundane would inspire great work. This was what she'd thought, initially, but so far her supplies remain in boxes and all she does on her days off is watch Netflix and eat rice cakes with sharp cheddar and pickles, waiting for Gabe to come home. She blames her lack of inspiration on Cameron Hornby, partly, and the shoppers generally. She's exhausted at the end of a shift, not by the physicality of the work, which is minimal, but by the generic interactions, the sheer quantity of them. So many faces appear before her over an eight-hour shift, so many expressions to compute, even though she does nothing with the data. It leaves her feeling a bit dead inside. She tries not to think what Arwen would say about her current state.

Jane watches Gabe move about the kitchen encased in spandex cycling gear. He's a bike courier Monday to Friday, but his weekends are dedicated to race training. She envies his motivation, his ambition, even if she also regards it as dogged and pointless. He doesn't have to work up to it, doesn't have to be in the right mood. He always wants to be on a bike, pedalling, or, when static, eating what will enable him to pedal more effectively. The second bedroom is hers for a studio. Maybe if she sets it up, it won't be so hard to get started, maybe the act of arranging her paints and brushes will be inspiration enough.

"Plug your ears," Gabe says. He flips on the blender and the fibrous mass of smoothie ingredients turns to liquid before Jane's eyes.

• • •

RECENTLY CAMERON WATCHED a documentary about the health benefits of a plant-based diet. He watched regular people shed pounds and ailments like nothing he'd seen before. It was staggering and persuasive and contagious. This week he's added lentils and tofu to the grocery list. He's underlined *kale* three times, written STARCH IS GOOD in capital letters.

"I'm all for it," Meg said. "But since when are you the cook in this house?"

"There's a website, with recipes," Cameron said, breathless with excitement and high blood pressure.

"What about cheese?" Meg said.

"It's basically an opioid."

"No kidding."

From Buy-It's kilometre-long refrigerated section Cameron selects a butter that isn't. Milk made from almonds. He's delighted to discover this alternate world of food he's been passing over for years. Not that he's never before heard of quinoa or farro. The younger women in the office where he worked until his slightly-ahead-of-schedule retirement had often brought Tupperware lunches brimming with curious mixtures, and he sometimes asked to be included in the recipe exchange that went around after a particularly fragrant meal overwhelmed the lunchroom, but only to feel like he was part of the team. In truth, he assumed each woman was hiding an eating disorder beneath her sprouted mung bean curry, and he continued to bring his unenlightened leftovers: pastas in cream sauce or oily beef stir-fry. How ignorant of him. How much time has he wasted? How much does he have left?

He surveys the contents of his cart. First his hyacinth, now this bag of short grain brown rice; Jane is going to have a field day. Cameron grins to himself. He imagines telling her: *The trick is taking meat out of the equation, removing that lump of flesh from the stereotypical dinner plate and reimagining it*. She will either laugh at him or see the truth in it, or both. Regardless, he's glad to have a rapport with her, to know that despite shopping in a warehouse with hundreds of people, it's still possible to make a connection. No doubt she has similar relationships with other customers, though he has yet to witness any. Every time he's waited in line, those ahead of him have filed through like robots. It's possible that what he and Jane share is unique, and Cameron feels grateful he can still entertain, perhaps even charm, someone half his age. Not in a romantic way, he doesn't think of her like that, but he does believe they have chemistry, a brain chemistry that goes beyond age and sex and class. Kindred spirits, that's what they are. Cameron imagines Jane seated at the dinner table with him and Meg, sharing one of his newfangled healthful concoctions and hours of easy conversation. It won't happen, but what if it did? Would their interactions have the same energy outside the store? Or is their banter best in small bursts? What if he did invite her over? Would she accept? Cameron feels a stitch of nervousness in his chest, a trill of possibility. He's reached the end of his list and so steers his cart, heavy with nuts, legumes, and three types of squash—the manifestation of his new moral code—toward checkout number ten.

IT'S JANE'S JOB to engage, to a point. It isn't exactly customer service—there's a counter designated for that—but she is required to be civil. Most of the time she's a step above civil: pleasant. Why not be pleasant? Why not make small talk with a person you recognize? Especially when it's more difficult to pretend not to. But if she thinks about it—as she does now with Cameron Hornby trying to catch her eye through the gauntlet of people ahead of him—it's mostly men she feels compelled to talk to. She can't think of a single woman who comes through her till, even regulars, who asks anything more than that she scan their coupons and dole out the requested number of bags. Sometimes a *hello* is exchanged that contains recognition, warmth in the eyes serving as non-verbal acknowledgement: *Look at us, caught in an existence that requires us to stand on opposite sides of a conveyer belt semi-regularly.* But it would shock her speechless if a woman asked where she collected the shell she wears on a chain around her neck or who she was with that day. And it would be beyond bizarre if a woman looked at her Buy-It nametag and decided to call her Janie. Who gives their cashier a nickname?

Now here's Cameron Hornby about to arrive in front of her, practically demanding intimacy. She picks up the service phone and, in a flat voice that sounds out across the store, summons relief to checkout ten.

CAMERON IS CERTAIN Jane sees him in her queue before being replaced by another cashier and disappearing through dark swinging doors marked *Employees Only*. When it's his turn, the new cashier, a baby-faced boy with dead eyes, does not congratulate him for remembering his own bags (as Janie surely would have), and Cameron sulks a little, cramming his bulk walnuts and tempeh bites into his slippery, packable sacks. He remembers her saying she'd recently moved in with a boyfriend. Maybe things aren't going well.

"Is everything all right?" he asks the boy cashier, handing over his credit card. Cameron's grocery bill is astronomical. He feels faint.

"Hunh?"

"With Jane. She left in a hurry."

"Dunno. Any bags?"

"No, I just—"

"Cash back?"

"Can I leave her something?"

"Over there," baby-face says, pointing to another line. He turns to the next customer, asks, "Points card?"

Cameron pushes his embarrassingly full cart over to the

Customer Service counter, which deals mostly with returns—spoiled milk, broken safety seals. When he reaches the front of the queue he sets the hyacinth, its flower grenade-tight, on the counter.

"Is something wrong with it?" asks an older woman in an apron identical to Jane's, with a name tag that reads Ellen. By older, he means close to his age.

"I'd like to leave it for one of your colleagues," Cameron says. "With a message, if I may."

"How nice," Ellen says and hands Cameron a Post-it note and a pen. He senses her skepticism, her belief in an ulterior motive, and feels his cheeks flush at the implication.

He writes: *Sorry I missed you. So much to tell you! I'm vegan now. Bet you weren't expecting that! Until next time … Cameron (Cam).*

"Don't worry, I'm not a creep," he says, sliding the flower and note across the counter, sniffing to pull in his stomach and correct his dejected posture to reflect that of a respectable citizen, a vegan.

"Okay," Ellen says. She turns away from him and places the pot on a shelf with other sad-looking items. He doubts the flower will make it to Jane.

JANE HAS HEARD that everyone in the United States is friendly, everyone talks to everyone else; apparently, they can't help themselves. She knows her city's reputation is the opposite, even within Canada. Arwen, originally from Toronto, once said she'd never felt so isolated as in Vancouver. "People actively look away instead of making eye contact, even when you're the only two passing on a deserted street." Maybe Jane's a product of this, her city's snobbishness and reserve. But surely even in the Midwest, where American charm is supposedly as offensive as their president, it's possible to dislike the look of a person and not necessarily be able to explain why. Surely there are some people with whom even the warmest of folk don't want to engage, not because of a crazed look, but because of a *feeling*.

Jane is having too many feelings, which is why she agrees to smoke up with Gabe upon arriving home from work. They huddle together on his punched-out couch, the one thing Jane would like to replace in the apartment, and she tells him about escaping her counter seconds before Cameron Hornby was set to arrive in front of her, about her subsequent feelings that she a) overreacted or b) is a victim of stalking. She watches Gabe read and reread the note. Jane would like him to offer an opinion, to provide a compass point, a direction for her to consider, but he knows better, and this, she realizes, is one of his best qualities. He's thoughtful and diplomatic and doesn't talk for the sake of it. But a measured response isn't what she needs right now. She needs validation, the kind she would get at her old house. If Jane had voiced these feelings in the presence of Arwen and her housemates, there would have been an immediate, visceral reaction. The note would have been passed around, commented on more savagely than necessary, and then burned in a Wicca-lite ceremony over the kitchen sink. They would have shared stories of similar encounters and assured her she wasn't imagining things.

Jane thinks about the many offices Gabe visits each day as a bike courier, delivering envelopes that require urgent attention and signatures. She knows he chats with the receptionists, all women. She knows some offer him baked goods and tales from their weekends. But do any of them feel burdened by his appearance in their foyers? Are any of them counting the seconds until he leaves?

"It's different," Gabe says, and Jane realizes she's been thinking aloud. "We're both doing a job, we're both at work. Your relationship with Cameron Hornby isn't balanced."

"There is no *relationship*."

"Well, there is. He's the customer and you're the employee tasked with serving him. He doesn't have to shop at Buy-It, he could go somewhere else, but he comes there for you, at least partly."

Jane shivers and Gabe lights another bowl.

"What should I do?" she says finally.

"Listen to your gut."

"My gut wants to slap a restraining order on his ass." But she knows there's no accusation she can make that would warrant one. Cameron Hornby's done nothing wrong.

Jane feels exposed on the couch, pushed up against a drafty single-pane window. They're on the second floor facing a busy street. She thinks pedestrians are looking up at them, gawking. She's also freezing. She rolls off the couch and onto the floor, starts crawling toward the bedroom.

"Wait," Gabe calls after her. "It's the pot, it's making you paranoid. I'll bring you a snack."

"Just come to bed." She continues on her hands and knees down the hall, past her boxes. Maybe she was wrong to move in with Gabe, maybe she never should have left her coven of Ayurvedic cooking and Friday night rom-coms. Maybe she's depressed, deeply depressed, because passing all of her worldly belongings she doesn't give a shit, doesn't feel at all compelled to unpack and integrate them with Gabe's, to make their lives fit.

Then she remembers it's February and it's been raining for five months straight. Of course she's depressed, the entire city is.

ONCE, AFTER A FEW drinks at a Christmas party, Cameron slapped his deputy minister on the ass and knew, immediately, that it was wrong. Of course he did. Of course it was. She gave him a warning look, that was all, and he nodded, backed away into the crowd, chastened. That was his worst but by no means his only instance of inappropriate touching, which makes it sound so much worse than it was. In general, his hands gravitated to his female colleagues' waistlines, not with sexual intent, but with compassion if someone was having a low day, encouragement if someone was on the upswing. Some women laughed and leaned in; others sidestepped him when they saw it coming.

"Right, right," Cameron would say, blushing a little and stuffing his hands in his pockets.

The first formal complaint was made by a young woman, young *person*, who preferred gender-neutral pronouns (another thing he had trouble getting the hang of) and whose shoulder he'd patted in passing one too many times. *They* simply did not like to be touched by anyone—male, female, or non-binary. It was unnecessary in the workplace, they claimed, and they were right. Despite Cameron's handsy reputation, however, everyone knew he wasn't a predator, didn't they? He was just a man from a particular generation that women, that *people*, were waiting (some more patiently than others) to go extinct.

The root of the problem, if you wanted to call it that, was that Cameron loved women. He wanted to be in their company. He wanted to be accepted by them. He'd never been at ease in the world of men, didn't enjoy sports or Scotch or profane humour, and his peers, sensing this, never tried to draw him in. He was an honorary member of Meg's book club in that he was allowed to attend the occasional meeting, but he tended to dominate the conversation, one of the reasons he'd never been fully embraced by his female peers either. And now that he's retired, he can't even pretend to be part of a tribe of women, to stand on its periphery and listen in on the conversations he so relishes about family trials and vacations and friendship woes. He's unmoored, a true outcast. He has Meg, of course, but after forty-one years she tolerates him in the way of an old dog, with a requisite pat here and there. Otherwise she leaves him to fend for himself, to follow patches of sunlight around the house and lap at his bowl. It's pathetic. He's pathetic. Or has been, until now. He's about to upset his routine, thank god. He's armed with a new knowledge: heart health and the myth about protein. He has finally figured out how to exhume his best self, haul that part of him made dormant by dairy and meat into sharp relief, and that's sure to attract attention, from women and men alike, as he radiates from every irresistible, plant-based pore.

Home from Buy-It, Cameron exorcises the fridge of many small bits of mouldering cheese and purges the freezer of beef patties and chicken breasts. He pours what's left of the milk down the drain, reciting, "Blood and pus, blood and pus," those lesser-known though equally abundant enzymes contained in a carton of the white stuff.

"What will I have in my coffee?" Meg asks, entering from the hallway.

"Coconut milk, or soy milk, or any of the other ones." Cameron waves at the table where he's left the groceries.

"I'm very attached to my coffee," Meg says.

"Just try it. We're trying this. If it doesn't fly, then it doesn't." Cameron is already feeling overwhelmed and unsure. Maybe this is a terrible mistake. He's also starving. He grabs a bag of almonds and rips it open, stuffs a handful in his mouth. Then a banana. Better. Much better.

"How was your girlfriend today?" Meg asks.

"Don't call her that," Cameron says. "I didn't see her." He doesn't feel like explaining how Jane left in a hurry at the sight of him, because that's essentially what she did, if he's honest with himself.

"Touchy," Meg says. "I'm heading to aquafit with Barb. I'll be hungry afterwards, so get cooking, maestro."

Meg leaves and Cameron continues with the kitchen restructuring, replacing the bad oils with the good and pouring hemp hearts and chia seeds and flax seeds into glass jars. The vacant look Jane cast in his direction before she disappeared from the till replays as he wipes the crisper clear of onion skins and bendy carrots. It was as though she didn't recognize him or wished she didn't. It was so out of character, yet what can he really claim to know of her character? They talk for a total of five minutes once a week. He jams the crisper back into its slot and kneels for a moment, panting. It could be he's missing the point, some very key point. It wouldn't be the first time. But he has never touched Janie anywhere, on the shoulder, hand, or arm, he's certain of it. His touch, his criminal touch. Jesus, when did warmth and kindness, expressed through innocent physicality, become so fraught? Where did this trend toward the reptilian occur? He's convinced that's not what's at play here, not with Janie, but something about it feels the same as those final days in the office. Shame washes through him like a tide of sewage.

THE FOLLOWING SATURDAY Jane has no plan other than to repeat her escape from the week before. It's not sophisticated, but it's the best she can muster. She doesn't see Cameron Hornby enter the store, nor does she sense his eyes on her at any point. For a fleeting window between 8:15 a.m. and 10:30 a.m. she decides he hasn't come; he got the message, her telepathic restraining order. Everything feels possible today because sunlight blares through the glass doors and people are moving quickly in an effort to get back outside. Jane is already planning to take her break among the smokers in the produce-strewn delivery lane, to stand with her face tilted skyward for the vitamin D. Maybe she'll even dig through her boxes of supplies later, set herself up. Amazing what a little sunshine can do! Her break is at eleven a.m., and then it's downhill to the end of her shift.

But she's not so lucky. At 10:34 a.m. Cameron Hornby materializes in her queue, behind two people with baskets, not cartloads that take longer to ring through and would thus afford her more time to make her getaway. He's snuck up on her, kept himself hidden until now. She's furious at how trapped she feels. She sees her hands shaking when she starts in on the first basket and refuses to make eye contact with him. She scans a few items, pauses, and then picks up her phone and calls for relief.

"Would you like the special offer?" she asks the customer.

"What is it?" the woman asks warily, already taking hold of her bags.

"A potted hyacinth. Just show your receipt to the checker at the door."

The woman mutters something about allergies and hurries off. Jane starts on the next basket, glancing around for her backup. She picks up a loaf of bread and checks the expiry date.

"Are you sure you want this?" she says. "The expiry is today. There's mould on the crust."

"Seriously?" says the customer, a young guy setting out what looks like the ingredients for brunch.

"I can run and get you another one. It'll just take a minute."

"I'll skip it, thanks."

"You don't need bread? It looks like you need bread," Jane says, gesturing to the rest of his groceries: eggs, bacon, mesh sack of oranges.

"Yeah, no. I don't have time."

She puts the perfectly fine loaf aside and scans the remaining items. No one is hurrying toward her till to relieve her.

"Would you like the special offer? It's a—"

"Nah, all good." He taps his card and, like that, he's gone, and Cameron Hornby takes his place before her.

"Bags?" she says with steely neutrality.

"No, thank you," Cameron Hornby says, and in those three words Jane can tell something has shifted. His voice betrays hardness, hurt, resolve. It's a weird combination of feelings to have, but along with the panic, she experiences a surge of pride; her intuition about him wasn't wrong.

IT ISN'T EASY to act like you don't care, Cameron discovers when he comes face-to-face with Jane at her till. But this is a test. If he gives nothing, will she? She keeps her head down and whips his groceries across her scanner without pause. Cameron moves to the end of the belt to begin bagging. Eventually, she'll have to tell him what he owes, she'll have to ask him how he'd like to pay. In other words, she'll have to speak to him. Jesus, this silence, so immature. Cameron feels a bubble of irritation swell in his throat. He bags his items with care, slowly. He will not be rushed; she cannot hurry him away. He watches her scan a brick of tofu once, twice, three times, then pick up the phone and call for a price check. She's almost reached the last of his items, at which point they will both stand there awaiting the price of tofu, that contentious soy product so beloved by some and so maligned by others. Will she really say nothing about his bag of chickpea flour and tub of cashews? Oh, the wonders of cashews! If only she cared to ask.

There, she's reached the last of his groceries, and he's almost bagged everything she's hurled toward him and they're still waiting for the price check. He will not falter, he will not leave; he wants that tofu. He also wants desperately to say something, anything to break the uncomfortable silence, but he mustn't waver. If she won't speak, neither will he.

"TAKE IT," JANE says finally. "Put it in your bag." If she gets fired for giving away a lump of tofu, so be it. She has a line of people waiting, and Cameron Hornby standing stubbornly at the end of her belt is more than she can handle.

"I will not," he says. "That's theft."

"Your total is $176.70. How would you like to pay?"

"Is that with or without the tofu?"

"Never mind. It's your lucky day," Jane practically growls. She can feel the next person in line, a woman her mother's age, growing impatient.

"You haven't told me about the deal," Cameron Hornby chirps smugly. "The free hyacinth. And I don't believe you've said thank you for the one I left you last week, when it wasn't free."

Jane barks out a laugh, incredulous. "Thank you?"

"It's the appropriate response upon receiving a gift."

"Actually, I believe it's inappropriate to leave such gifts." There, she will match his superior tone. She will not become hysterical, though it's exactly how she feels inside.

"I liked you, Jane. I enjoyed talking with you, human to human. But I can see I was wrong about you."

"Do you know this man?" the woman next in line asks.

"I thought our conversations were real," Cameron Hornby says. "What we shared."

"Any sharing was purely accidental. On my part, at least." Jane is surprised to feel tears spike her eyes. She hears Arwen telling her to pull it together. "Your *hyacinth* is in the trash."

Cameron Hornby may not be a serial killer, a bona fide stalker, a groper, or even a liar. But he is, Jane feels certain now, the kind of man who's been indulged most of his life, coddled. Is there art in this, Jane wonders? It seems unfair that there might not be, that she simply has to endure this petty guilt trip because of her station in life. *Station*, such an archaic term for one's status, but it feels right given her apron and bus pass.

"He gave you a flower?" the woman next in line asks.

"She looked like she could use some cheering up," Cameron Hornby interjects from the end of the belt. "I bought it for myself, for my wife, really, but I changed my mind and gave it to her."

"Young women today are quite something," says the woman, shaking her head slightly.

At last, Jane's co-worker appears for the price check.

"Never mind," Cameron Hornby says. "I'll buy my tofu elsewhere. It isn't even organic." He thrusts his upper body into his cart and veers toward the exit, away from Jane. He won't be back; she knows this for sure. Will he make a complaint? She doesn't care. She turns back to her register.

"Quite something," the woman murmurs again, and Jane deflates a little. Flicking the woman's items across her scanner—a pack of single-serving yogourts, a slab of white fish on blue Styrofoam, a bag of Ambrosia apples—Jane wonders what the hell she's talking about. *Young women today are quite something.* How so? she wants to shout. Say what you mean! She can't tell if the woman's being critical or admiring, if she's shaking her head in amazement or disdain. Arwen would know, or she would act as though she did. She would fire off some retort, shut down this woman's passive-aggressive murmurings.

Jane hands the woman the card machine.

"I have cash," says the woman.

"Cash? Who carries cash these days?" Now it's Jane shaking her head while the woman counts out her bills and change. She sets the money in a neat pile, gathers the handles of her shopping basket, and turns to leave, shoulders rounded by the burden of groceries or age.

Castoffs

Even after a ruthless cull, Lena realizes that, at forty, she has enough footwear to last her until she dies. It isn't that she has so many pairs, just that she has enough; impossible she'll wear through all that rubber and tread in the next however many years.

"You're having a bit of a revelation, then," Helen says, shouldering the bag of Lena's shoes to her car. "About your mortality."

"No," Lena corrects her. "About *shoes*."

"Shoes, but not *only* shoes."

"You know I'm not great at small talk," Lena says, changing the subject to the women gathering on a rooftop patio in Helen's townhouse complex with their own sacks of clothing and shoes. "Especially now I'm not drinking."

"What?"

"I texted you."

"Thought you were joking."

"Is this an attempt to pawn me off on new people?"

Helen is the executive director of a reputable arts organization. She keeps the books tight and the staff in line while maintaining an attitude of caring for their personal and professional growth. She does not suffer fools, and Lena often wonders why she puts up with her. Maybe Helen has room for one fool in her life.

"Don't overthink it," Helen says. "They're just women like you who've cleaned out their closets and are looking to go home with a new top and have a bit of fun."

"You're right," Lena says. "You're always right."

"Not always. Most often."

Helen is an artful driver. She manoeuvres in and out of lanes selfishly, skillfully, without appearing to provoke the ire of other drivers. Lena feels safe with Helen at the wheel. She'd like to skip the clothing swap and be Helen's passenger for the evening. They could take the Sea to Sky to Whistler for dinner, coast home with the setting sun.

"Guess what?" Helen says as they swoop into her parking stall. "Old people often wear orthopaedics. You might need another pair yet."

"Right again." Lena sighs.

THE FRONT DOOR to the host's home is open, and the rooms are empty but for a couple of teenage boys playing video games in the living room, sunk into the upholstery like lesions on an otherwise perfect face. The place has the same layout as Helen's, only backwards, and maybe in reverse since Helen has a ground-floor patio, not one up in the sky. Lena is discombobulated and out of breath, her shoes and sweaters and whatever other garments she crammed into shopping bags, clothes she at one time thought would make her life better, fuller, proving now that not only had they *not* done as advertised, but also that they'd made it worse by draining her bank account and making her complicit in the exploitation of factory workers in places like Bangladesh. She stops, mid-flight between the bedrooms and the rooftop, and crumples onto the stairs.

"What are you doing?" Helen snaps. "We're almost there." It's true. The hatch to the "sky lounge," as Helen calls it, stands open. Beyond it, the unselfconscious laughter of women in mid-life ready to pick through Lena's clothes.

"Is this about the shoes again?" Helen asks. "Or is it possibly about Jack?"

"Jack can go to hell," Lena says reflexively. Of course, Helen is right, Jack is mixed up in the stew of self-hatred and existential sorrow churning in Lena's gut. How could he not be? In fact, he's the stew's main ingredient, has been for the past twenty years.

"Right," says Helen. "This makes more sense."

"And I'm not drinking," Lena says.

"No one *has* to drink."

"But I really want to, that's the problem. One of the problems."

"What do you want me to say? I don't think a glass will kill you, if you want it that badly."

Helen leaves Lena on the stairs and disappears through the hatch. There's a seismic rupture of greetings as Helen makes her appearance among the women, Santa Claus with her sacks of clothing. Lena wonders: how is it a person doesn't realize she's destroying her life until she's inspecting the ruins, turning the rubble over in her hands?

Lena and Jack decided not to have children and instead do all the things people without children are free to: travel, eat dinner after eight p.m., sleep in on weekend mornings, go to the cinema (not the Cineplex). And because they had no children to enroll in private school, or gymnastics, to clothe or shod, they also had the time and money to learn about wine. They had the means to travel to learn about wine. Jack did the learning and Lena did the drinking. Jack was interested in the chemistry, tannins, and terroir, while Lena was interested in how in love she was with Jack after a glass of Amarone. But it was impossible to stop at one glass, rarely at two, most often three or four. All through her thirties Lena woke feeling like shit. She thought that's what came with being an adult; at a certain age, youthful resilience fell away, and the world assumed its true aura of shitiness, palpable and throbbing before she even opened her eyes. Every night she and Jack shared a no-less-than-twenty-dollar bottle, watched an episode or three in a true crime series, and then Lena fell into a sweaty, restless slumber, only to wake puffy and headachy the following morning. She kept a supersize bottle of Tylenol beside the bed. Somehow Jack didn't need them. He could wake, shower, and leave the house without coffee in his veins. It wasn't fair. Alcohol was poison to Lena in a way it wasn't to Jack.

Helen reappears in the doorway with another woman.

"Coming or going?" says the woman.

"I have a choice?"

"Lena," says Helen sternly. "Meet Nancy. Our host."

"Actually," says Lena, "we've met."

"Oh, I didn't realize ..." says Helen.

Lena stifles a sour laugh and doesn't bother to explain how exchanges like this sum up her life: *We've met. Oh, I didn't realize ...* Lena is apparently so unremarkable that people she's met once, twice, sometimes three times, whose first and last names she can recall with ease, have no memory of meeting her. In recent years she's given up saying it—*we've met*—opting instead to perform the introduction anew, all while trying to see herself reflected in the other person's eyes: what about her is so easy to discard? Throwing it back at Nancy, as she's just done, is rude. She doesn't want to be rude.

"Are those your kids in the living room?" Lena says.

"If they ignored you and wore expressions of disgust at nothing you could discern, then yes, they're mine," Nancy says.

Lena engages her wobbly legs. She takes hold of the railing and pulls herself up. "You must have had them young."

"My second was a geriatric pregnancy," Nancy says. "I was thirty-five."

"What does that make us now?" Lena asks.

"Crones, hags, shrews," Helen practically sings. "Take your pick!"

"Battle-axes." Nancy cackles and whisks the last of Lena's bags out to the sky lounge.

THE METHOD IS THUS: each woman takes a turn being the Vanna White for the contents of her bags. She holds up one garment at a time, detailing the size and brand. The first among the group to speak up and claim a garment becomes its new owner. Simple. However, if two women want the same item, there's a makeshift changeroom set up where they must each take a turn trying it on and appearing before the group, who will collectively decide on whom it looks better. Unpleasant. When this situation entangles Lena, over a boxy black blazer, she immediately relinquishes the garment to her competitor. It's because she's sober. If she were drinking, she'd gamely engage in the spectacle, and this new sobriety makes her question her longstanding perception of herself as a generally lively and outgoing individual. She's also anxious at the prospect of having to be the spokeswoman for her discards. She can't bear the thought of these women appraising her taste and perhaps deeming it insufficient, unsophisticated, or cheap. Maybe she'll go to the bathroom and slip out before it's her turn. They can tear through her bags without her present, mock the cropped chinos and floral blouses. Why so many floral blouses? For a while she was convinced the manufactured splotches of colour distracted from the natural splotch that was her face, the tender smears of purple beneath her eyes, the flush of panic that sprung over nothing—when trimming her fingernails or loading the dishwasher—and radiated heat from her chest to her scalp. (A hangover symptom, she now knows.)

But these women aren't interested in mocking her. They're here for a glass of wine and a dress if they're lucky. They are teachers and doctors and entrepreneurs. They are mothers and wives and dog owners. Lena sits beside a woman who recently lost a staggering amount of weight, and a husband—Lena is unsure in what order, but she can guess. This woman sits beside another who acts like the formerly overweight woman's personal shopper, snapping up clothes for her friend's newly slim body. The personal shopper rarely jumps on any of the items for herself. Lena is put off by her business-like approach to the evening; she isn't here for a good time, she's here to update her friend's wardrobe. But what's so wrong with that, really? The friend appears baffled by each item selected on her behalf. Is she unconvinced it will fit? Does she not like the style? A jean jacket is on the table. Old Navy. Small.

"Hilda will take it," the personal shopper calls out, stepping into the circle to claim it on Hilda's behalf. Hilda sits dumfounded as the items pile up on her lap.

It's Lena's turn next. If she had a drink or two in her system, she could do it with a flourish, or the playful tone of a car salesman, and she wouldn't care if there were no takers. More for the donation pile, no big deal! But in her sober state, her true state, she's self-conscious of her rejects—tinge of yellow in the armpits of a white T-shirt she tossed in, a little too much pilling on an acrylic-blend sweater. The table set with drinks and snacks is farthest from where Lena is seated. She doesn't even have time to fail at her sobriety for the sake of her upcoming performance. *This should not be a big deal,* she coaches herself. *They don't care about the sales pitch. They just want to see what's in the fucking bags.*

Jack is somewhere in the city possibly shouldering a bag himself, a diaper bag to be exact, one belonging to a newish baby, Lena knows from Facebook. This baby will need many pairs of shoes over his lifetime: rubber boots, fuzzy slippers, sneakers, water shoes. A little over a year ago, Jack traded in his wine subscriptions for a pair of neon-green trail runners. He joined a group that trained together to run off-road ultramarathons, up mountain switchbacks and down scree slopes. He came home from these training runs exhilarated and exhausted. He talked about his running crew while Lena prepared pasta and sipped wine. His new friends sounded single-minded, driven to succeed in ways she had no interest in. Lena had never viewed her body as a tool to be honed and purposed, pushed to experience any sort of limits or discomfort. In hindsight, she realizes she was meant to follow Jack's lead. She was supposed to seek clarity in the pain of her exertions. Or at least give it a try. But on those days when he chose to hurl himself at the world, she preferred to fold into herself on the couch with a book. At first, Jack claimed he was doing it for them both, trying to shift them toward more healthful versions of themselves. "We aren't kids anymore," he'd said, after presenting her with a pair of running tights and a merino wool top, because it was cold up in the mountains. "Am I behaving like a kid?" Lena snapped at him from a heap of cushions where she was crumpled with a thriller and a headache. Had he and Angela already started running shoulder to shoulder at this point? Had they begun matching their strides to be close to one another up the fire roads, before they hit the single track of the forest trails where, at any moment, the rest of the group might disappear around a tight bend, and they could be alone under the moody, complicit trees? Jack left Lena, married Angela, and had a baby they named Sage, all within a year. It embarrassed Lena that she hadn't seen it coming, and it stung to be the one who was left for her failure to grow. If she'd laced up the trainers and huffed her way up a mountain, would it have made any difference? She'll never know.

"Lena, you're up," says Helen. Another woman has just finished showcasing at least a dozen pairs of low-rise jeans, in varying shades of denim, that she purchased before accepting that the style didn't suit her body type. The woman is doubled over in hysterics, laughing at her own stupidity. No one has claimed a single pair; it's common knowledge they don't suit *anyone's* body type in the over-forty crowd. This strikes the woman as even more hilarious. "How did you all know?" she hyperventilates. "Who do I think I am?" Lena thinks she must be drunk. She's embarrassed for the woman, also envious. She, too, wants to abandon the sour normalcy of her thoughts, tilt them toward something more rare. But the tilt is a lie, and she's trying to remain upright these days, no longer shirk the true jab and sting of existence. When did being alive become so hard?

"I have a bunch of stuff in here," Lena mumbles, pointing to her bags. "None of it very exciting."

"We'll be the judges of that," snorts the jeans woman. "Unless you've brought a sack of crop tops to pair with my jeans, there's got to be something we want."

Lena's hands shake a little as she extracts the dress she bought in Lucca, Italy, in a shop the size of her bathroom. It's constructed—this is the correct word for such a piece—of a rich fabric that swings seductively about the knees when walking ancient streets arm in arm with your love, after a long meal comprising many exquisite courses in the central piazza. But Lena doesn't say this in her sales pitch. She doesn't have to sell it. The personal shopper snaps it up for the newly thin Hilda.

"That was easy," says Lena, more to herself.

"Wear it with the jean jacket," the woman instructs Hilda. They clink glasses of rosé, and Lena aches for that sweet kick to her nervous system. It's been fifteen days since she had a glass of wine. She hasn't joined a support group, though she does follow a few sobriety accounts on Instagram and, depending on the day, finds their inspirational stories and advice uplifting or cringeworthy. Fifteen days is not long. She could relapse without even admitting that's what it was. She could walk over to the table, pour herself a glass, and no one would stop her, not even Helen.

Lena rambles through a selection of black sweaters, then the floral blouses, a stack of precisely folded pants, and finally the running gear, still sprouting tags. Each item finds a home. Lena catches Helen looking at her in the waning light. It's a look of evaluation, as if Lena is one of the items up for grabs and Helen is considering putting her name in. It's another reason Lena drinks: people's eyes and the unknowable judgments behind them. Helen raises her glass to Lena, perhaps in congratulations for having survived the spectacle of sharing. *See*, Helen says without words, *not such a big deal*. Lena rolls her eyes at her friend: *You're right, you're always right*. Aside from obsessing about not drinking, Lena's felt so good the past two weeks she can't understand why she didn't try it sooner. Jack had finally used it as the excuse to leave her, after claiming he'd done all he could to help her. He hadn't done anything, really, except abstain and disappear evenings and weekends on his epic courting runs.

Nancy sparks a coil running down the middle of the coffee table. Flames spring to life and the tipsy women in the sky lounge are delighted. Lena remembers she hasn't offered up the sack of shoes she hefted up all those stairs.

"Wait," she says, interrupting the private conversations beginning to bloom along the interlocking sections of patio furniture. "I have shoes."

"Shoes!" the women sing.

"We love shoes!" Nancy shouts.

"I have too many," Lena says.

"Don't we all," says Helen drolly.

Lena pulls out a pair of sleek black ankle boots with pointed toes, then a pair of tan, mid-calf boots that suggest an impractical stroll in the desert. Everything is size eight, which excludes several women. But Hilda is still in the running and Lena is invested in her makeover now. She slides pair after pair in Hilda's direction and feels a pulse of satisfaction watching her exclaim over the fit each time.

"Even after getting rid of these, I still won't have to buy another pair until I die," Lena says.

"But you will," says Nancy.

"Maybe," says Lena. She feels lightheaded now, having divested herself of her old skins. The fire illuminates the women's faces and she's able to observe them more freely from the shadows. There's youthful laughter paired with falling jaw lines, microbladed eyebrows, and thinning lips. There's Helen streaked with too much bronzer and highlights showing grey at the roots. There's Nancy with a pronounced stoop, more noticeable in profile, pouring herself a glass now that her hosting duties are winding down. Lena feels warmth toward all of them, and at the same time cold disconnect; they won't remember her beyond tonight. She goes inside to find the bathroom, passing the teenage boys in the living room, still lost in their alternate world of video games. She washes her hands and doesn't look in the mirror. Lately, she's recognized her grandmother's eyes in her own, specifically her drooping eyelids in their outermost corners, that gradual curtain call. Toward the end, her grandmother's eyes had reminded Lena of a grey whale's, the way the great mammal appears to understand everything it beholds—herring ball, plastic bag, moonlight—in relation to all else in the universe, and without judgment. That's how Lena's grandmother looked on Lena from her deathbed, and it was the last true gift she received.

Lena decides not to return to the sky lounge. Helen will be irritated, accuse her of indulging antisocial tendencies, but she'll get over it. It isn't too far to walk home now that she's unencumbered. *Guided meditation, forest bathing, hot cups of tea.* These are just a few of the rituals that might help a person overcome her cravings. It's only been fifteen days. There's an unopened bottle of Malbec in the cupboard, smooth and medicinal as cough syrup. No judgment. There's a baby somewhere in the city, a baby she might have wanted, being cared for by a man she stopped trying to know because she was so busy unknowing herself. Lena hasn't come away from the swap with one item, neither scarf nor sundress. Good. Things are distractions. What else can she purge? The excavation has begun. Or is it an exhumation? *Call a friend, try knitting, learn to play the ukulele, journal.* It's all a little airy-fairy.

A block from home Lena can feel the twist of the corkscrew in her hand and anticipate the happy dulling of her senses after the first glass. She can also see beyond to the headache and self-loathing she'll wake to tomorrow morning. Her brain is awash with rationalizations and excuses. To each her own. Fill your boots. Old habits die hard; just try not to die of old habits. Her feet aren't sore—she's wearing a pair of trainers Jack would approve of, not that she seeks his, or anyone's, approval, except maybe Helen's—and she could walk a while longer. A nearly full moon has risen. A few assertive stars. No one she passes knows or recognizes her. She hardly knows herself.

Rescue

Riley spies the boy one rainy night in February. She's on her final walk of the day with Jeju, a pandemic mutt she'd summoned from Korea back in April, during the first lockdown, and who hadn't arrived until November, during another one. The shelter, where Jeju had spent his first year of life, relied on good-willed travellers to assume responsibility for a dog while in transit, and since no one was travelling and goodwill was hiccupping toward extinction, dogs had become yet another product subject to shipping delays, like laminate flooring, smart speakers, and Veuve Clicquot. Even when Riley finally got the call that Jeju was being loaded onto a plane the next day, she still had a hard time believing he would ever materialize in Vancouver. It only became real once she, Brock, and Lola were standing masked outside arrivals at YVR.

"Are you sure this one's ours?" she'd said to the customs agent who'd delivered Jeju's crate by luggage trolley—rather unceremoniously, too, Riley thought, for the wait they'd endured.

"Looks like," the agent said, glancing at the paperwork.

Inside, huddled against the back of the crate, was a creature much larger and more wolfish than he'd appeared in his online pictures, reeking of urine, and peering back at Riley with glossy, fear-filled eyes.

"What's wrong?" said Lola, ever attuned to Riley's emotional twitches.

"Nothing. He just looks a bit different."

"Because he's real," Brock said.

The customs agent turned, signed documents in hand, and marched carefree through the terminal's automatic doors. Brock was right; Riley had never cared for a dog, and faced with the responsibility, the actual mangy, shedding being, she felt inadequate and embarrassed by her hubris.

"Did you think he'd be wagging his tail, happy to see you?" Brock said. "He was drugged and shoved in cargo for ten hours."

She'd never admit it, but yes, Riley *had* thought he'd be wagging his tail, ready to slather them in kisses. He looked like such a fun-loving guy in his pictures. His tongue hung out in a few, as if he'd just had a good romp with some pals. He practically smiled. Yet here he was, nearly unrecognizable. What had she done? *I'm working from home, let's get a dog!* Stupid, kneejerk woman.

"You're broody," Brock said, back when she'd first embarked on her search on Petfinder.com, a massive database of dogs in need of homes. "What you really want is another baby, but we both know that's not happening."

No, it wasn't happening. Riley had crossed the forty-year line and had almost died in childbirth with Lola. Was she broody? Maybe. But not for a human baby. Riley claimed the dog was for Lola, a companion for an only child, a means to knock her slightly askew of centre stage, to teach her responsibility, empathy, when in fact it had little to do with these things. The dog was for Riley and Riley alone. It was as if some intuitive force—her own animal nature—knew that Jeju would be her salvation in the months to come. And hasn't he been just that? Not only a mental distraction—the figuring him out—but also a physical one. A dog's exercise is a state-sanctioned, guilt-free activity, and conversations—at a distance, sometimes masked—with other dog owners, with neighbours she never knew existed, have provided Riley with the social outlet she hadn't known she needed.

Now, nearly four months later, she's like so many others in her neighbourhood, those being dragged about by leashes, or coaxing their dogs to walk on leash, stopping to exchange phone numbers for experienced trainers, brands of motivating treats, and curious canine behaviours. One of which, for Jeju, involves yelping if the leash so much as grazes the side of his body. Riley is usually careful to not let this happen, though it has, just now, because she's distracted by a ground-floor apartment's kitchen window and, more specifically, by a boy crouched on the tabletop manipulating a large jug of milk and a box of Shreddies.

Jeju barks and tries to bolt, but Riley grips the leash in time to prevent a mishap. Still, his thrust has power. Pop in her shoulder, tweak in her elbow. "Jesus," Riley snaps. *Adopt, don't shop*: the slogan of all animal rescue organizations, encouraging potential dog owners not to fork out thousands for a purebred and instead take in a stray. Riley agrees, in theory, but in practice she sometimes wishes she were ambling along with a ubiquitous Labradoodle, a dog who didn't bark wildly at people in embrace, flapping raincoats, or babies harnessed to their parents' chests. And yet, here she is. Here they are, she and Jeju, passing through a pedestrian-only courtyard, between two buildings in the sleeting rain. Riley takes this route not only because Jeju's nose insists upon it, but also so that she can peer into other people's homes and lives, especially since no one is allowed inside other people's actual homes or lives anymore. It gives her a reassuring sense of community to see people sitting before their screens, bent over a steaming pot on the stove, drinking wine and staring back at her. She's waved, twice, to different people who seemed to catch her eye, though neither returned the gesture. Maybe they didn't see her? Hard, though, not to see a person wave. Harder still for two people not to see. Nevertheless, it's comforting to know there's a community out there, existing in a kind of cryptobiotic state, ready to be revived when the time comes, if it ever does.

Riley reaches down to stroke Jeju's head. He shrinks from her touch. In their family unit, he prefers her, which isn't saying much. She looks in at the boy shovelling cereal into his mouth and waits to see a parent enter the room, scold him for being on the table. Jeju stands with the leash taut, at full extension, telling her it's time to go. The boy cups the bowl in two hands, drinks, then hops down and dutifully puts the cereal box on the counter, the milk in the fridge. He switches off the light and the scene falls dark.

Riley waits for the leash to slacken before proceeding, a tactic meant to mitigate pulling. It doesn't work. Jeju yanks her toward a bush and sniffs its leaves passionately. Occasionally, he'll lick delicately at the urine already deposited there—to know its owner more intimately, Riley read online. Disgusting, Lola has remarked. Is the boy home alone? He's too young. Maybe six years old. It's eight thirty p.m. He should be in bed. Lola is nine, not much older. Chances are she also isn't asleep yet. Over the past year she—along with the daily case counts and the slow re-openings followed by even swifter shutdowns—has worn her parents down and now sleeps in their bed, the "big bed," as Riley and Brock's California king is called.

"She won't sleep with us forever," they've reassured one another more than once. "Who knows how this is affecting kids?"

Riley had hoped Jeju might help get Lola back into her own room, be her sleeping companion, but so far, daughter and dog have yet to bond. Jeju has, more often than Riley would like to admit, growled at Lola if she approaches with too much verve, and Riley's uncomfortable leaving them alone together. She doesn't think Jeju would do anything, but what does she know about dogs, let alone ones hauled off the streets of Korea?

Riley looks back at the apartment. Maybe the boy is being raised by a single parent, a healthcare worker doing grueling shiftwork, sweating and exhausted in one of those medical HAZMAT suits. That's why he's home alone. *You don't know he's alone*, she imagines Greta, her best dog-park friend, saying. When she and Greta walk together, usually a few evenings a week, they often speculate about the lives of the people behind the windows they pass. Greta, though, never lets Riley get too carried away. *The boy's parents, or parent, are probably in the other room, just out of view.* Greta is the rudder forever pushing back against the wild sea of Riley's imagination.

"They should get blinds, then," Riley mutters, "to stop weirdos looking in."

DURING THE FIRST lockdown, back in April—before Jeju and before Greta—reports of animals roaming deserted streets—a herd of Kashmiri goats in a seaside town in Wales, coyotes in San Francisco—had read like a silver lining to Riley. The earth and its creatures were getting a break from the constant assault that is life alongside humankind. With no one driving or flying, the air was cleaner; without boat traffic and gillnets, fish populations were able to flourish; animals reclaimed their disrupted migratory routes. In her isolation, Riley scrolled these stories gleefully. They were a particular balm following the death of Takaya, the lone wolf who'd wended his way through farms and backyards and eventually swum to a small island off a populous neighbourhood in Victoria on Southern Vancouver Island. He'd lived there for eight years, alone. The curious public were banned from going ashore while a local biologist documented Takaya's life, circling the island in her kayak, capturing video of him in regal repose or feasting on seal carcasses. When the CBC aired the biologist's documentary about Takaya's solitary life, the wolf became an instant celebrity. Riley, like much of the population, was mesmerized by his noble gait, his coat's distinct black and tan markings, his perseverance without a pack. She rooted for him in his quest to attract a mate; his howls into a wilderness that was no longer wild were in fact a song for a female to join him. Apparently, one tried, stood on shore howling back to him, but she wouldn't brave the two-mile crossing.

Then, in January, as the world slid from its rails, Takaya abandoned his island refuge and swam back to Victoria, leading conservation officers on a chase through residential neighbourhoods. He was eventually tranquillized and relocated to nearby wilderness where, predictably, he was shot. Takaya was rumoured to have been killed by a woman with a history of trophy hunting. She received death threats. If Riley'd had any clue where to send one, she would have added to the mob's chorus. In her anguish, she considered having her students—more than a hundred combined in her first-year composition classes—write one as an assignment. She wrote her own first: *You scum of the earth, I'm coming for you. No gun. I'll wring your neck with my hands ...* The letter went on like this for several pages, panting and circling itself. Riley imagined mailing over a hundred death threats at once! But to what address? Could she create a website and post them online? She'd be fired in an instant.

"It's a blip," Brock said of the animals cavorting across the planet. "This pandemic is a blip."

"A blip is better than nothing," Riley sniffed. She was already teary, having announced at the dinner table that their application for a dog—from Korea, where animal rescue organizations claimed dogs were slaughtered for human consumption—was successful. "If we don't celebrate our blips, what do we have?"

Lola furrowed her brow, swept her fork through her food. Riley knew she should pull it together, but this world—what a shitshow, what a wasteland of doom.

"We're getting a dog, for real?" Lola said.

"For real," Riley said with too much emotion.

"I'm not picking up poop," Lola said. She was punishing Riley for her display of weakness. Suck it up and be the adult, was Lola's tone. *Who's ultimately going to have to inhabit this shitshow, this wasteland of doom?* And she was right. The children were always right. "No poop pickup for you," Riley said firmly. It was the least she could do.

• • •

THE NEXT EVENING, Riley meets Greta on the seawall at their appointed time. Greta might have been a Scandinavian queen in another life. Tall and solid, with excellent posture and dirty blonde hair that swings down her back in a rope that could pull ships to safe harbour. Tonight, she looks like a giant gnome, sausaged in an ankle-length down coat with a conical toque perched atop her ears. Milo, her Maltese, springs about her ankles, a Mexican jumping bean. Riley tells Greta about the cereal-eating boy the previous night, and about her imagined conversation with Greta.

"That's exactly what I would've said," Greta says. "You don't even need me now."

"Oh, but I do," Riley insists. "I need you to rein me in."

"Is that what I signed up for?"

"No one else even applied."

"Did I have a choice? My dog fell for yours, despite his foul temperament."

As if on cue, Jeju growls at Milo's efforts to cajole him to play.

No rain tonight, but the temperature has dipped and the seawall glitters beneath the streetlamps. Jeju leads the charge, knows his evening route. Greta links her arm through Riley's and they're a couple out for an evening stroll. They pass a shuttered pub on the pier, reduced to one sliding window through which a person can purchase off sales. It glows like an apothecary, like hope in medieval times. A friend made in adulthood, without children as the binder, is as rare as Takaya slipping through your backyard. Almost a year since his death, Riley still finds herself addressing his killer: *You selfish sack of shit, the next time you go hunting a pack of wolves will chase you down, tear you apart limb by limb, and gorge on your flesh.* There was much speculation about the hunter, a name accompanied by images on the internet of a heavily tattooed, frosted-lipstick-wearing woman kneeling, rifle in hand, over a slain lion and other majestic creatures rendered into limp sacks of fur and organs by her bullets. Riley is livid that no news story or website has ultimately disclosed—and she has waded through the putrid sludge of many comments sections and forums—where Takaya rests. A statement from the Ministry of Environment reads that his body was returned to the Songhees First Nation for proper burial, but the word *body* stopped Riley. If *all* of Takaya had been returned, why did they specify *body*? Did that murderer have his coat splayed on her rumpus room wall?

Riley is ranting, the horror story spilling from her own frothing muzzle, entrails and all, to Greta, who'd caught snippets about Takaya's death on the news, but almost immediately on its heels came shelter in place, N95 masks, and Zoom.

"Do we want to go this way?" Greta asks. Jeju has steered them from the seawall into a maze of apartment buildings. The path narrows and wends around a pond with a footbridge that Riley once tried to coax Jeju over but stopped when she noticed his tail had sunk between his legs.

"Wait," Riley says. "We're here." She pulls her phone from her pocket in case she needs to document something. A telling detail. A scrap of evidence.

The boy's kitchen window is dark, but light cast from an adjoining hallway reveals the shapes of appliances inside. The apartment is separated from the footpath by a mere strip of dirt. Riley can walk right up to the glass if she wants. Next to the kitchen is a poorly fenced patio covered in moss and leaves. Curtains cover the sliding glass doors and TV light seizures behind them.

"Well?" Greta says. "The only neglect I see is a building in need of paint."

"Maybe he's alone, watching TV."

"Or someone else is. Or they're watching together."

Milo begins to bark at the wind stirring branches above. Jeju starts up in response.

"We're causing a scene," Greta says, pulling Milo down the path.

"I'm just curious ..." Riley says. She takes a few steps toward the kitchen window.

"What are you doing?" Greta hisses.

"It's tidy."

"Which means an adult keeps it that way. If someone sees you—"

"I'm picking up after my dog."

"People could be watching."

True. The courtyard is surrounded by condominiums with floor-to-ceiling windows, but Riley isn't doing anything wrong. She's letting her dog sniff and pee, and sometimes that means getting too close to someone's home, but what can you do in a city, with a dog? Mostly, people watch to make sure you pick up after it, which she does, without fail.

"I'm leaving," Greta says.

If someone should flick on the kitchen light, they'd see a woman with her nose nearly pressed to the glass. She would frighten the boy in her hooded anorak; any sane adult would come after her. Box of Shreddies on the counter, a few Pokémon cards scattered on the table. Riley strains to see into the hallway: bare wall, beige carpet. She slips her phone back into her pocket and knows she shouldn't feel disappointed. The boy hadn't looked unhappy eating his cereal on the table, only a little too independent for a child so young. Riley still fixes all of Lola's snacks and meals. Learned helplessness. She isn't doing her daughter any favours.

Greta waits beneath a streetlamp on the far side of the courtyard. Riley can feel her friend's hostility in the way Greta doesn't take her arm. Shaking her head, she says, "Too much."

"I have a bad feeling. Sometimes you need to listen to your gut."

"Everyone has bad feelings these days. It's a hard time for *everyone*. You need to manage your stress. I meditate. I walk the dog."

"I also walk the dog."

"You need to do more."

Greta strides furiously and Riley hustles to keep up. The dogs pull on their leashes, ready for home, for bed.

"I'm sorry," Riley says when they're nearly back at their starting point. "I get carried away."

"It's too much," Greta says, taking Riley by the shoulders and giving her a little shake. "Sometimes *you're* too much."

"I know."

"Try not to be so reactive. Slow down. Take a breath. Promise?"

"Promise." Greta releases Riley and blows her a grudging kiss before disappearing into her building's entranceway, a queen bestowing forgiveness on a commoner.

THE NEXT MORNING Jeju refuses his morning walk to school with Riley and Lola. He sits on the couch, hindquarters shaking. Riley clips the leash to his collar and tries to lure him with treats.

"He's so neurotic," Lola says, parroting Brock.

"Be kind," Riley says. She removes the leash and he folds in on himself, tucks nose into tail. Rather than seeing Jeju as an ally, Lola continues to view him as her adversary, complicating her life, funnelling attention away from her. Riley comes to his defence more and more frequently. They are becoming two teams within the household: Riley and Jeju versus Lola and Brock. Is this what having two children does to a family? It doesn't help that Jeju continues to shun Lola's small gestures of friendship—a cucumber slice on the floor beside his bed, a squeaky toy flung about to entice him to play. Her most recent overture—an ear rub, last night—was met with a sharp bark.

"No!" Lola had shouted at Jeju, wounded by his rejection, and frightened, too. "Bad!" She'd stormed into the kitchen where Riley had been trying to make dinner and leave the two of them to fumble their way toward some understanding. "What's *wrong* with our dog?"

"He's just scared," Riley rushed to answer. "He's still decompressing from his previous life. We need to give him space, move slowly." She was making excuses again. Not exactly blaming Lola, but clearly siding with Jeju. She knew how it sounded.

Brock, thus far silent on his laptop at the kitchen table, finally spoke up. "He's had plenty of space. It might be time for a family meeting."

"Since when do we have family meetings?" Riley said.

"Now, I guess. I'm just not sure he's the right fit. Jeju. For our family. This isn't what having a dog is supposed to be like. We shouldn't have to tiptoe around him."

"Do we tiptoe?" Riley said.

"Maybe not you. But Lola and I do. Definitely. The question is: Does he enrich our lives?"

"That's a big responsibility for a dog. Don't saddle him with our happiness."

"You know what I mean."

"I'd say he does. He does *enrich* my life."

"Lola? How about you?"

Lola had been sitting quietly on the stairs, listening to her parents. She was sensitive to tone and became upset when they spoke to her in anything other than a singsong and carefree way. She'd once accused Riley of speaking "sternly" to her, as if it were the worst thing a parent could do. She didn't like it when they spoke sternly to one another, either.

"He doesn't play or cuddle," she said. "He's mean to me."

"He barked at you," Riley clarified.

"That's mean."

"Not all dogs are cuddly."

"I think we should consider rehoming him," Brock said.

"Rehome is a sanitized way of saying 'get rid of,'" Riley said to Lola, even though she knew her daughter understood.

"Lola's frightened of him. Don't you see?"

"Yes, I *see*."

"Try to be objective about this."

"I don't want to get rid of him," Lola whimpered. "I just want him to be nicer."

"That takes time, Lo," Riley said. "We've only had him four months."

"I'm not convinced," Brock said. "I think he is who he is. It's not his fault and it's not ours."

"Your mind is obviously made up."

"I'm telling you what I think. I know you're attached to him. I can see that, but we live here, too."

The family meeting ended in a stalemate. Riley said nothing more because she could feel her temper rising. She was furious at Brock. It was a conversation they should have had without Lola. She felt attacked, cornered, and was convinced Jeju felt the tension, too. He had retreated to his bed after rejecting Lola's ear rub. He felt bad about snapping at her, Riley was certain. And now he wouldn't leave the house. He's worrying himself sick.

Lola and Riley walk to school in silence.

"Have a good day," Riley says perfunctorily, at the junction of two paths where she leaves her daughter to walk the final fifty feet alone.

"Uh-hunh," Lola says, tromping off to meet her friends. She betrays no trace of wanting, or even considering, a parting hug, an even further punishment for Riley since they both know it's she who craves it most.

Without Jeju, Riley avoids the dog field and walks home along the seawall. A flock of overwintering Canada geese have settled in the middle of the path, unfazed by joggers and strollers, hissing half-heartedly at dogs. Riley navigates their piles of grassy, toxic poop—goose pâté, as some dog owners refer to it. Thankfully, Jeju doesn't have an appetite for it. Riley couldn't talk to Brock privately about their failed family meeting last night because they'd all wound up in the family bed together. What she'd wanted to remind him of were the few private sessions they'd had with a trainer whose expertise was working with rescue dogs. "Jeju has street dog DNA," she'd said, "and all its accompanying instincts for self-preservation." It struck Riley as profound. *Of course* he was anxious and wary; look where he came from, how his relations were treated, or mistreated.

"So there's no hope?" Brock said to the trainer.

"Depends what you're hoping for."

"A dog that doesn't growl when I sit next to him on *my* couch would be nice."

The trainer gave Riley a look, a raised eyebrow that said: *Your work extends beyond my jurisdiction*. She said, "He'll never be a lap dog, if that's what you mean." *Remember?* Riley wanted to say to Brock. *We knew he'd never be a* normal *dog.*

At home, Riley sees that Jeju hasn't touched his food, likely hasn't left the couch. She turns on her computer, readying herself for class. Jeju's haunches quake in waves. His eyes follow her every move. She takes a moment to sit next to him and scratch his ears. He presses his head into her hand. Why couldn't he do that for Lola, or Brock?

Today Riley's lecture is on persuasive writing. Once the students have arrived in their mostly black squares, she shares her screen to reveal a sample of her own writing (unconventional, she knows), an impassioned and precisely written plea addressed to the premier of British Columbia to end the wolf cull immediately. She reads it aloud so that her students can hear her conviction, supported by her word choice, her varied sentence lengths, her rhetoric. Upon finishing, she expects neither applause nor conversion, but her heart is racing a little and a head nod of approval from even one of the three squares in which actual human heads appear would be welcome. She asks if any of them know the story of Takaya, the lone sea wolf. Silence. Then a few thumbs-up emojis appear in the chat. She posts the link to the CBC documentary about Takaya, then an article about his death, to demonstrate how she came to know and care about the issue. Do they care about issues? She encourages them to share some of the causes they might feel moved enough to write about. Slowly, a few type: crypto, minimum wage, Britney Spears, Covid sucks.

"And you're more than welcome to jump on my bandwagon if you're at a loss," Riley says. "In fact, I encourage you to. The wolves in the province will thank you. I will thank you—"

Riley feels a tap on her thigh. Jeju's nose. His very discreet and gentle way of telling her he needs to go outside. "Oh," she says, startled and still on camera. She hadn't heard him get off the couch. "I'm so sorry," she tells her students, "I have to sign off. The rubric is online—" The black squares have already begun to implode. Riley closes her computer and heads for the door, where Jeju waits, still shaking and with apologetic eyes.

"It's okay, sweet boy," she says. She clips the leash to his collar, and he scurries out the door as if danger is on his heels. He walks a few feet, then freezes and looks back at Riley.

He does this for a couple hundred feet then stops, seemingly unable to go any farther. Riley stoops and collects him in her arms. She carries him to a patch of grass where he often relieves himself. He sniffs, tail tucked, still quivering, and starts to turn circles, pawing at the grass the way an animal might to prepare a final resting place.

"What are you doing?" Riley asks, bewildered. He paws and paws, not with any vigour, but with a kind of sad determination. Then he circles the patch of earth and lies down. "No, no, no," Riley says. "Not here." She gathers him in her arms again and carries him to a hydrangea bush he's fond of drenching. Nothing. She returns him to the couch.

Riley meets Lola at three p.m., in the same spot she left her that morning. Lola doesn't comment on Jeju's absence and Riley knows it's intentional. Riley, spiteful, doesn't offer to take Lola's backpack. They walk home in silence. *Does he enrich our lives?* Mother and daughter aren't speaking. Husband and wife are at odds. Do you just toss a pet if it doesn't immediately live up to your expectations? Disposable. Replaceable. Breedable. Eatable. Isn't it these attitudes toward animals, at least in part, that have landed humankind where they are now, in the Anthropocene?

"I need to take Jeju to the vet," Riley says. "Do you want to come or stay home?"

"Alone?"

"I won't be long, and Dad will be home soon."

"What should I do?"

"Watch a show. Whatever you'd do if you weren't alone. Except eat."

"Why not?"

"I don't want you to choke. I'll be half an hour, max. You can call me."

Lola nods gravely.

"Or you can come with me," Riley says. "Maybe you should."

"I don't want to."

"It's fine, you'll be fine. And don't answer the door."

Riley loads Jeju into the backseat and takes him to his least favourite place. Because he won't eat, she hasn't been able to get the requisite anti-anxiety medication into his system beforehand. And because of Covid, she isn't allowed to go inside with him. Jeju's look of betrayal as she hands his leash to the technician is undeniable. The tech tugs him over the threshold and tells Riley to wait for their call before returning, probably around midnight. In the driver's seat, Riley leaves her mask on so that she can weep freely. What has she done? She should have insisted on staying with him. Her phone rings. Is it the vet already, calling to tell her they can't examine him, he's too aggressive, he's bitten someone?

"You left her alone?" It's Brock.

"Lola? Is she all right?"

"Yes. But you just don't do that. She's only nine."

Riley breathes a sigh of relief.

"I knew you'd be home soon."

"What if I'd been delayed?"

"She didn't want to come with me."

"You make her come. That's what kids do, they go with their parents whether they like it or not. Are you crying?"

"No. I'm sorry. You're sure she's okay?"

"She's hungry. She says you told her not to eat."

At home, Brock and Lola go about their evening as if Riley's not there, practising Lola's words for a spelling test tomorrow, running her a bath. Are they ignoring Riley or is she shutting them out? Is it always this way, and she doesn't realize because she's busy catering to Jeju? Without him, she has no purpose, no partner. And without him she has no reason to go for her evening walk, which she's now trained to need as much as him. Despite a headache beginning to pulse at her temples, Riley pulls on her coat and boots and slips outside. She follows the same route she would if Jeju were with her, along the seawall, past the darkened pub, the water taxi dock. The wind gusts, and the boats anchored out in the Creek jostle on the waves. Across the water, downtown flaunts its glassy teeth. Walking at night feels pointless without Jeju, possibly unsafe, too. There's no one else about. Jeju is no guard dog, but he's ready to bark at anything that strikes him as amiss, particularly once the sun has set. Her poor creature, alone in a kennel. He will not forget this betrayal.

There are no homes to peer into tonight. Everyone has their window coverings pulled; it's as if Riley's being shut out on purpose, for making assumptions about their lives, for letting herself in without an invitation. She deserves it. All of it. The cold shoulders from Brock and Lola, Greta's frustration. She's testing everyone she loves, pushing them to their limits. It's childish of her. She'd thought she was handling this global crisis, if not well, then at least adequately. Hasn't she adapted to online work, stopped touching her face? Doesn't she wash and mask up without complaint?

Riley's about to turn homeward when she remembers the boy. She'll just stroll by and take a quick peek. There will be nothing to see, but what if? She puts her head down and walks briskly toward the courtyard. It strikes her that she hasn't mentioned her obsession with the boy to Brock. Possibly because she knows what he'll say. Like Greta, he'll dismiss her so-called gut instinct as misguided, or just call her nosey. Which means that, on some level, she knows he's right. As she knows he's right about Jeju. The animal has only agitated their marriage, their family. Their jaws are set in anticipation of his next misstep. But this is where she and Brock diverge. Riley doesn't believe an animal is capable of misstepping. An animal's behaviour is pure. It has no ill will, no vendetta. It responds to outside forces based on instinct. In rain, it seeks shelter. Faced with hunger, it seeks food. In loneliness, companionship. Jeju doesn't want to be the rift in their family. If he wants anything at all, it's peace. They are the cause of any rift. Therefore, only they have the power to mend it.

Riley turns into the dark courtyard. The boy's kitchen windows are lit, and he's there, at the table, looking out into the darkness. It's as though he's waiting for her. Maybe he's looking out for a parent he expects home soon. Maybe he's been frightened by a sound and is bravely investigating. Riley keeps her distance—without Jeju she has no excuse to get too close—but she slows her pace, and, as she passes his sightline, she raises a gloved hand and waves. For a beat, their eyes meet. He's a little older than she first thought, closer to Lola's age. The boy flips Riley the middle finger and runs from the room.

THERE'S NOTHING MEDICALLY wrong with Jeju. The bloodwork reveals a minor potassium deficiency, but nothing that would cause shakes and lethargy. Whatever it is, it's in his head. The vet prescribes patience and a thunder shirt to apply calming pressure, and hands Riley a seven-hundred-dollar bill. Despite the sedation, when Jeju is released from his kennel he musters a valiant display of affection, nudging Riley's hand with his nose and permitting her to rub his muzzle. How could they possibly rehome him now when he's starting to trust them? *Trust you*, Brock would argue.

It's after midnight when Riley and Jeju make their entrance. Instead of disturbing Brock and Lola, Riley pulls back the covers on Lola's neglected twin bed. Jeju follows her into the room, legs trembling, and rests his chin on the mattress. Riley lifts him onto the bed and slips under the blanket, makes a concave space with her body. She pats the spot.

"Here," she says, but miraculously he needs no coaxing. Jeju curls himself into a tight donut next to her and Riley is lulled asleep by his animal warmth and the undiagnosable tremors passing through his body and into hers.

That night she dreams of Takaya. She's his companion on the island, before his death, and she's also a wolf. Takaya shows her how to eat mussels from the rocks at low tide. The shells splinter effortlessly under her canines and the prized goop melts down her throat. Four legs are better than two. Riley moves with a fluid grace she's never experienced in human form. She slides around the trunks of weather-stunted oaks on Takaya's heels, pauses to sniff dried moss on a hillock. It's a perfect existence, this waiting for the next tide or storm or season, this fierce attention to nature at the same time as being a part of it. Until Greta appears, wrapped in her long down coat despite the blazing sun. This is not a friendly visit. Somehow Takaya knows, bolts. But Riley's limbs are fixed. She watches as Greta, stone-faced, somehow stately as ever, pulls a rifle from inside her coat, positions Riley in her scope. Riley shouts, pleads, but of course no human sound issues forth, only an anguished howl. Greta, unmoved, pulls the trigger.

Riley wakes with a headache welded to her skull like an iron crown. She's cold beneath Lola's duvet. Shivers spasm through her torso. It's dark. Early. She needs help in the form of Tylenol, but the prospect of leaving the bed and moving through the chilled house is excruciating. Jeju has relocated to the floor, sprawled with the confidence of a dog who knows his place in the world. He lifts his head from the carpet to acknowledge her wakeful state. She can't make out anything else in the dark—for instance, if he's still trembling—but his alertness suggests a positive change.

It's Saturday morning. When Riley hears Lola begin to stir, she calls to her. Lola enters swiftly, guard not fully in place for the day. Riley asks her to fetch medicine and a glass of water, which Lola does obligingly, before realizing the inconvenience of a sick mother.

"You make pancakes on Saturday."

"I'm sorry. I just can't."

"Do you have it?"

"Maybe. You should probably stay out of here."

"It's my room."

"I know."

Brock enters next. "Who's going to walk the dog? He won't go with me." It's true. Jeju won't leave the house without Riley. He'll allow Brock and Lola to clip the leash to his collar, but he won't budge once it's on.

"I'll wait for the drugs to kick in. Then maybe I can do it." Walk the dog, such a simple chore on the surface, but one so fraught in real life.

Riley falls back into a tortured sleep and dreams of nothing. Her subconscious is a flat grey sea, sour and dying. Takaya has abandoned her. All the animals have. Her own coughing wakes her. The house is still. Brock and Lola have left her to die alone. Fair enough. She hasn't been an exemplary mother or wife lately. She's been running loose through the neighbourhood spinning her wild tale of neglect and abandonment. In times of yore, in the village, she would be the gossip, sowing scandal and discord among her neighbours. She would live alone in a shack with her mangy mutt, her sole companion. She'd reserve the best cuts of meat for him and allow him in her bed.

Jeju. She calls out for him. No click of nails across the living room floor. No stealth appearance in the doorway. She rises slowly, her whole body aflame now, the earlier chills extinguished. Where is he? Where are Brock and Lola? Riley finds her phone on the kitchen table, an email marked urgent on the screen. It's the message she knew, in her gut, was coming: her faculty head requesting a meeting. She reads, *Some students have expressed concern* and *encouraging them to write threatening letters to government officials and hunting associations*. It's overreactive on the part of the administration, but she's relieved to no longer be anticipating the reprimand. Riley closes the email and looks outside to the boulevard, where her eyes fall upon a most unexpected tableau: Brock and Lola, Jeju on leash. Maybe she's hallucinating. Another fever dream. Somehow, they've gotten him out the door. Coaxed, lured, yanked, who knows? There they stand, her pack, gathered on the grass, recalibrating the hierarchy, sniffing the wind, and preparing to move on without her.

The Getaway

We took the ferry after work on the Friday of the Remembrance Day long weekend and arrived at the vacation rental—a palatial beachfront home with five bedrooms, a chef's kitchen, and an outdoor hot tub—in tandem with what news reports had dubbed a "bomb cyclone," a weather system that would accompany us for the duration of our stay.

"Why not just call it a storm?" Alicia said, as we piled our bags into the vaulted foyer. Suitcases filled with slippers, bathing suits, sweatpants, good jeans, rain gear, and runners. And shopping bags filled with alcohol, weed gummies, coffee, tea, non-dairy this and gluten-free that. All the fine-tuned particularities that comprised each of our forty-something-year-old tastes and that would be essential to sustaining us during this weekend sidestep from routine.

"Because it's *not* a regular storm," Crystal said. "It's one for our age."

"Which is?" Alicia said.

"Dire," Crystal said. "I hope this isn't news to you."

I hung my coat and slid from my rubber boots. The house smelled strongly of cedar, as though someone had spritzed an essential oil seconds before we entered. A bowl of apples, cold to the touch, sat on the kitchen table. Gaping windows reflected our arrival back at us. Alicia, Crystal, and I were the first carload to make landfall. God willing, the others would be along shortly. I was already exhausted by their back and forth. On the ferry they'd disagreed over where to sit for the two-hour crossing—forward lounge or cafeteria. They'd quibbled over podcasts for the car ride, and then talked over the celebrity interview I eventually chose as their tiebreaker. Then they gave me conflicting directions to the house, each bent over Google Maps while I piloted through sheeting rain. I hadn't asked for this—a bachelorette, or hen party, or whatever you chose to call it. I'd done it the first time around and was content to skip it. Tofino was a long way to travel for only two nights; I'd rather have gone out for a lavish dinner in the city and slept in my own bed with Daniel.

"You get first pick of the rooms," Alicia said.

"I'm sure they're all fine," I said.

"A few of us will get bunkbeds," Crystal said.

I didn't want a bunkbed, so I climbed the floating stairs to the second floor, the two of them tripping at my heels. The skylight above us was awash, as though our invisible host were stationed on the roof with a hose. Prints by renowned

Indigenous artists decorated the walls. The lights, as we flicked them on, cast the orange hue of firelight. It was a stunning home I couldn't imagine anyone truly inhabiting. Why would a person need so many rooms? I'd always lived in cramped city apartments with too little counter space, a poorly ventilated bathroom and, if I was lucky, a balcony or cinderblock patio, room enough for a café table and chairs. Recently, I'd moved into Daniel's downtown condo, and although it wasn't much larger than my own, it did have an ensuite—an extravagance—and the high ceilings and grand windows overlooking English Bay made it feel expansive, as though, if I chose, I could waltz out onto the ocean's glittering grand ballroom floor.

"Here," Alicia said. "The primary." She was already inside, rolling across the bed.

"Wait!" Crystal shrieked. She turned on her phone's flashlight and yanked the sheets from one corner of the mattress. "Let me check the seams. It's just common sense."

"This place doesn't have bedbugs," Alicia groaned.

"Bedbugs don't discriminate," Crystal said.

There was a jacuzzi tub in one tiled corner of the room. More picture windows that would, presumably, with sunrise, reveal a grey expanse of beach.

"Well?" Alicia said. "Do you like it?"

"I don't need all this," I said.

"No one *needs* it," Alicia said. "But we want this for you."

I felt bad for thinking that wasn't entirely true, that my upcoming nuptials were just a convenient excuse to escape their families. But even if that were the case, or partly so, who could blame them? These women, all of them, had busy lives: full-fledged careers of mid-life, children needing transport to various sports tournaments, aging parents to care for, pets to attend to. Some had partners to help them, others didn't. It was no small feat to organize and gather this weekend, in celebration of me and a relationship I sensed some weren't thrilled about.

"I don't want to sleep in here alone," I said. "One of you has to stay with me."

"Can all three of us fit?" Crystal said. She hopped onto the bed next to Alicia. "Here," she said, patting the mattress. "Lie down."

We lay in silence, listening as the bomb cyclone pressed against the house on all sides like a fierce animal asserting its power.

"If Mallory Martin could see us now," Alicia said.

Alicia, Crystal, and I had met in university, in a women's anthropology class presided over by a professor with a near-ecstatic following. We, too, became converts, and over the years continued to invoke her name—Mallory Martin—as a kind of feminist prayer when we found ourselves in difficult life situations, when we needed strength, or sometimes just as punctuation, our own private version of *amen*.

"This could work," I said.

"Who gets up to pee the most?" Crystal said.

"All of us," Alicia and I replied.

• • •

THE SECOND CARLOAD of women, those who'd caught a later ferry, wouldn't arrive now until tomorrow. We learned by text that, shortly after I'd white-knuckled along the twisty two-lane highway in the dark and driving rain, a landslide had flushed down a streambed, halting traffic in both directions. Road crews wouldn't be able to clear the debris until morning. Our friends would spend the night in Port Alberni.

"The climate crisis is real," Alicia said, pulling a white bath robe over her bathing suit.

"Why now?" Crystal said. "Because it's interrupted our weekend?"

"Exactly," Alicia said.

"Ignore her," I said.

We were preparing to brave the weather in the name of the outdoor hot tub. It was partially covered by the roof's overhang, but the storm surged from all angles and there was no way to avoid an assault. We fumbled into the water, clutching canned gin cocktails.

"This is the life," Alicia said, squinting against the rain. She wore her thick blonde hair in two long braids and, over the years, had gained thirty pounds, but to my eyes she looked the same as when we met. Crystal, too. Though she'd gone grey early, she was still knotted and thin in her athletic bikini, her thinness now a result of triathlon training as opposed to the metabolism of her youth.

And how did I appear to their gaze? My own hair had thinned in the last few years, so I wore it cropped, and lately I'd given up makeup, except for mascara and, depending on the occasion, lipstick. My eighteen-year-old daughter, Glory, was forever suggesting products I could use and improvements I could make, but I just didn't see the point. Daniel called me his "natural beauty," and if he was happy with how I looked, that's all that mattered. We were getting married in a small ceremony at the Teahouse in Stanley Park on the winter solstice.

Daniel was nine years younger, and this would be his first marriage. I hadn't pushed for a wedding. Even after he proposed, I told him I was content living together, but he'd insisted on the ceremony, and to please him, I said yes. I hadn't realized that in doing so I would alienate my daughter and cause so much side-eye among my friends. Although my upcoming wedding was the reason we found ourselves together now, it was a topic that so far hadn't been addressed directly—neither on the ferry nor in the car—and Alicia and Crystal's avoidance made their opinion all the more stark. I wished the others hadn't been delayed. Buffered by the guaranteed noise that came with more women, it might have been possible to ignore their disapproval. And I wished Glory had come. She'd snubbed my invitation, which hurt because I genuinely thought she'd enjoy a weekend away with her mother and a bunch of women, two of whom she considered aunts, intent on having fun. Glory still hadn't RSVPd to the wedding.

• • •

INSIDE, I LIT A fire in the living room's woodstove while Alicia set out charcuterie and Crystal struggled to connect her phone to Bluetooth.

"Unfortunately, the decorations are in the other car," Alicia said. It was the first mention, albeit roundabout, of our supposed cause for celebration.

"That's a relief," I said.

"The penis straws were for *all* of us," Crystal said, giving up on the speaker and dialling in the local station's Friday-night DJ.

We were still wrapped in our robes. The hot tub and gin cocktails had made me sleepy. I did and didn't want to know why my friends were so uncertain about Daniel. Did they simply think we weren't compatible? I'd always considered myself a good judge of character, but might love have dulled my intuition?

"Cards Against Humanity?" Crystal said, pulling board games from a cabinet. "Better with more people," she answered herself. "Scrabble?"

"Let's eat," Alicia said, popping a bottle of bubbly.

I noticed Crystal drinking water and taking only occasional sips of champagne. She no doubt had plans to run before Alicia and I woke. I regretted the current of awkwardness in the room. That I should feel even a little uncomfortable in the presence of two of my oldest friends confounded me and made me feel at fault. I drank my champagne quickly. Alicia tapped at her phone and Crystal stretched on the carpet in her swimsuit.

"He doesn't want children," I said. "If that's what you're worried about."

Crystal was bent over, hands touching the floor. She looked back at me from between her legs. Alicia's eyes rose from the glow of her phone. They remained still, unspeaking, so I was compelled to fill the silence.

"I know something's going on," I said. "You two aren't as subtle as you think. There's a vibe. There's *been* a vibe almost since I introduced you to Daniel, and definitely since the wedding announcement. I told you I didn't even want to get married. It's his thing."

Alicia and Crystal looked at each other. Crystal rose from her folded position and pulled on her robe.

"We were going to wait for the others," she said.

"Because we want you to know it isn't just us," Alicia added.

"For real?" I said. "Is this an intervention disguised as a bachelorette?"

Alicia's phone pinged in her hand. She read the text and said: "Glory says hi."

"Glory?" I said. "My Glory?"

"The one and only," Alicia said.

"Why is she texting you?"

Alicia shrugged. "She wanted to know we arrived safely."

I sensed there was something more Alicia wasn't telling me. I thought back to her silently tapping away on the ferry. She'd asked me where Glory was staying this weekend, while we were in Tofino. With her dad, I'd replied. About two months ago, as Glory and I packed and prepared to move in with Daniel, she had, instead, decided to go live with her dad, even though it would lengthen her commute to the city college by an hour each direction. I hadn't told Alicia or Crystal before now because I was still coming to terms with it myself. Daniel's condo offered Glory a spacious room with a million-dollar view, close to everything she was used to. Why she'd choose her father's mildewed townhome on a traffic-heavy artery perplexed me. Alicia's phone pinged again.

"Now she wants to know how you're doing," Alicia said.

"Tell her to ask me herself," I said. "I *also* have a phone." But, in fact, I'd silenced it. Daniel hadn't stopped texting and calling since I'd left. I knew Alicia and Crystal would think his behaviour overbearing. We were still in the early days of infatuation; I couldn't expect them to remember how that felt. "Tell her I miss her," I said. "I wish she was here."

Crystal shoved her hands into her deep robe pockets. She said, "Maybe you're starting to understand why she can't be here?"

"Not really," I said, defiant. I felt myself heading down a familiar path. I had, at inopportune moments throughout my life, exhibited a tendency to argue for the sake of it, to push for something I didn't believe just because—because those around me believed the opposite so vehemently. It had happened once in Mallory Martin's class. I was mortified every time I recalled her lecture on female genital mutilation. The class, most of us ignorant of the barbaric practice before that day, were rightfully horrified to learn the particulars of the procedure, not to mention the physical and emotional aftermath. For some inexplicable reason, I raised my hand and asked if we weren't viewing the practice through a Eurocentric lens, if we really had the right to judge cultures and traditions other than our own so harshly. Even as I was speaking, I felt ill about the impression I was making. When I finished formulating my supposed point, the room stayed silent for a few long seconds before I was, justifiably, piled on by my peers. I could still recall the looks of confusion and disgust on my new friends'—Crystal and Alicia's—faces, and the look of dismay from our professor. That day, Mallory Martin asked me to stay after class and, once we were alone, asked if I really believed what I'd said. Was the evidence from Human Rights Watch and the World Health Organization not enough for me? It was, I cried, of course it was. At the time I didn't know what I was reacting to, but now I recognized it as a biological compulsion toward denial. The refusal swam in my blood. And I sensed it lurking now, as my friends tried to turn me toward something I didn't want to see.

"There aren't any decorations in the other car, are there," I said.

"No," Alicia and Crystal said in unison.

A sound started then, and at first I thought it was coming from inside me, an alarm trying to drown out whatever it was they were about to say, or a scream slowly building in my chest.

"Do you hear that?" Alicia said. The wail rose above the bomb cyclone's ceaseless pummelling of wind and rain. Crystal opened the patio door. The wail entered the room, mournful and urgent.

"It's coming from the beach," Crystal said. "I think it's a tsunami warning."

"No way," Alicia said.

It was the air raid siren I'd only ever heard in movies, the one that sent people fleeing to underground bunkers.

"We have to go," I said. I grabbed the car keys and shoved my bare feet into my boots.

"Like this?" Alicia said, flapping her robe open and closed.

"Yes," I said. "Now."

"But where?" Crystal said.

"There's an evacuation route," I said. I'd seen signs on our drive in, directions to higher ground.

We didn't lock the door. We didn't take food or water. We were barely clothed. There was dark irony in the fact that we wore swimsuits as a tsunami heaved toward us. I turned from the forested driveway onto the two-lane highway in the direction of town.

"How is this happening?" Alicia said. "Is it happening?"

I rolled down my window to admit the siren's haunting warning in the distance.

"There's no cell coverage here," Crystal said. She found the local radio station again, but no special news bulletin assaulted us, only the same dancehall mix we'd left playing back at the house.

"Why is no one else out?" Alicia said. "Why are we the only ones evacuating?"

She was right. The road was empty when it should have been packed with cars wending toward refuge. As we approached town, vehicles remained hunkered in driveways and diners were visible through restaurant windows. A few people smoked under an awning outside the local legion. I turned up the road toward the emergency reception centre. Its windows were dark. I parked in the gravel lot and stepped from the car. Alicia and Crystal followed. The siren had stopped, but the storm seethed on.

"Maybe it was just a test," Alicia said. "Somehow we're the only ones who didn't get the memo."

"A bomb cyclone *and* a tsunami?" Crystal said, laughing cautiously. "What are the chances."

I felt ill. "Could you just ..." I said.

"Now?" Crystal said. "Here?"

"Fine," Alicia said, facing me in her white robe like some sort of high priestess. "He condescends to you—"

"To all of us," Crystal added. "He doesn't like women."

"And he's said things to Glory," Alicia said. "She didn't want to tell you. She doesn't know how."

"That's insane," I said reflexively, more in reaction to

Glory's not being able to talk to me than to Daniel behaving as they claimed. I'd seen the way he looked at her, of course I had, but I looked at Glory that way, too. She was young and beautiful. Couldn't a person be in awe of such beauty and not interfere with it, just let it be? "What things?" I said.

When we met, Daniel had swamped me with compliments, and I luxuriated in his praise after such a long dry spell. I didn't question it. Someone was finally appreciating me, and I was worthy of his attention. Not only was he in love with me, but he couldn't be without me. It felt good to be wanted—no, *needed* with such passion.

Alicia said, "He told her he was glad they'd be spending more time together once she moved in."

But Glory hadn't moved in. She'd gone to her dad's instead, and Daniel had gotten angry, said something about kicking a gift horse in the mouth, and that Glory was spoiled. I protested, but when Daniel pointed out how easy she had it—free room and board, tuition paid for by RESPS that her dad and I had dutifully built—I wondered if he was right, if I had failed to raise her to be responsible and self-sufficient in a way she would need to be to thrive.

"We're so sorry," Alicia said.

I wanted the tsunami to knock me off my feet and suck me out to sea. Had Daniel said I was a natural beauty, or that I had a face makeup couldn't help? Did he say he didn't want to intrude when I was with my friends, or that my friends were intrusive? Did I say I never wanted to move from his apartment, or did he tell me I couldn't? Without question, he hadn't wanted me to come on this trip, had given me the silent treatment in the days leading up to it, had told me he'd be hitting the strip clubs with friends for his bachelor party. How did I like that? I knew that if I checked my phone, I'd find notifications of multiple missed calls and a screen full of bitter text messages.

"I need to call Glory," I said. "Will she even talk to me?"

"Of course she will," Alicia said.

"You're her mom," Crystal said.

I'd argued myself into believing Daniel was a good guy and ignored the alarm on my friends' faces, on my own daughter's face. What kind of fool was I? I wanted to curl into a ball on the gravel and be left to suffer the elemental consequences. I crumpled a little, but Alicia and Crystal stopped me from falling. They wrapped their robed bodies around me. We formed a misshapen moon in the empty parking lot and staggered a little as the storm lashed our bare legs.

"Mallory—" Crystal said.

"Martin," Alicia finished.

Welcome to the Neighbourhood

It's all Erik hears about lately. Amanda wants the tent gone. She's called the non-emergency police line about it *multiple times*. Erik wonders if there are groans before dispatch picks up when they see her number on call display.

"What disturbs me is that you haven't even bothered," Amanda says. "And the fact that we don't have curtains..." It's a sore spot between them. When it comes to home decor, there aren't many things Erik's adamant about, but the lack of curtains is important to him. Drapery of any sort—sheer, velvety, or otherwise—would make their living room feel like a cave, ruin the effect of looking out onto trees.

"You seem to forget," Amanda says, "we have a six-year-old who runs around naked, and those trees are dying."

"I don't forget," Erik says. "I just don't think anyone's out there trying to look in at our uninteresting lives. And the guy's not really doing anything wrong."

"There are no *facilities* in those woods," Amanda says. "Where do you think he's doing his business?"

"Can we just agree that whoever he is, he's not camping in December for fun?"

"Obviously," Amanda says. "But I can see that tent from our deck, which means he can see into our home."

At last, their drinks arrive, and they sit back on their stools to allow the server room to place coasters and glasses before them. It makes Erik feel infantile somehow, being waited on. Amanda appears to love it; she smiles over-graciously at the server and coos, *Thank you*, like a benevolent yet condescending queen. In her youth, Amanda slung beers in many fast-paced pubs, and Erik wonders if she thinks that gives her the right. He looks toward the taproom ceiling, its rafters laced with at least a hundred lines through which various craft beers and ciders flow toward their taps, and waits for the server to leave.

"Let's toast," Amanda says. It's their holiday date night, after all, an occasion that required planning—booking the table and a babysitter—and a tradition they've maintained from their childless iteration as a couple, one that, Erik hates to admit, feels more obligatory than it should. He raises his pint glass to Amanda's champagne cocktail.

"Wait," she says, rifling through her purse for her phone. "Okay, now." They clink glasses while Amanda records a loop that will play in perpetuity on Instagram.

"We didn't toast anything," Erik says. Amanda is bent over the screen, captioning or hash-tagging, he presumes.

"What?" she says absently, without looking up.

It's been troubling Erik lately, the enthusiasm with which his thirty-nine-year-old wife has taken to Instagram. She was late to join the party but is wasting no time catching up. Later, he will read her caption—*Date night with my fella* ❤🎄— because, after all, he too has the app, but only to follow lifestyles he'll never experience: heli-skiers, fly-fishers, brew-masters. He never posts anything himself, but Amanda does, and this particular one will depress the shit out of him because, although he's the aforementioned fella, and presumably the heart is meant for him, or to signify their love for one another, especially, apparently, during the Christmas season, it doesn't feel that way from where he's sitting, beside her.

"I don't know," she says, finally, placing her phone face down on the table. "What's to toast?"

"Just about anything," Erik says. "Our health, our home, our daughter."

Amanda sips, purses her lips in concession. "Sure," she says. "To all of those."

Their high-top table is one of several tucked in a warm corner of the taproom, from which they have an expansive view of the restaurant, a renovated salt factory with high ceilings and long refinished tables presently crowded with glassware, elbows, and shiny-faced humans out for a little Christmas cheer. Theirs could be considered a romantic table. It sits apart from the others, flaunting its intimate flame, but

Erik feels isolated over here, excluded from the merriment, and he suspects Amanda does, too. He would like to take her hand and lead her to one of the staff parties going off the rails around them, push their night in a different, less predictable direction, one they might laugh about in the morning over coffee and Tylenol.

"I heard some gossip," Amanda says, "about the new family across the courtyard."

"Oh?" Erik says, not in the least bit interested.

"Supposedly their marriage is on the rocks, and moving here is a last-ditch effort to make a new start for their kids."

"Hard when everyone knows your business," Erik says. He's irritated with Amanda for getting sucked into the drama, for trying to pull him in, too. He won't go there.

"Something about infidelity," Amanda says nonchalantly. Erik looks up toward the rafters, all that beer coursing through the place, what a job it must have been to get it rigged up and running smoothly.

"Does it surprise you?" he says. "We're at that age where it either keeps going or falls apart."

"Seriously?" Amanda says. "You make a relationship sound like one of Olive's toys."

"I just mean, not all marriages have the longevity gene. You see it more and more." Amanda knows this. Why is she giving him a hard time? It's happening to friends of theirs, couples whose collapses could never have been predicted. Erik has a headache. The noise in the taproom is practically nightclub level. Who are all these people out on a Friday night? Young people who can sleep in tomorrow. "I'm going to the washroom," Erik says, but stepping from his stool, he buckles almost immediately. A bolt of pain shears through his back and he braces himself on the table.

"That's one way to change the topic," Amanda says. She's slipped from her chair to grab hold of his elbow.

"My back," Erik says, wincing.

"Indeed," Amanda says.

"I think it's just a tweak."

"That's what you said last time, and you were out of commission for three days. Might be time for me to trade this model in."

AT HOME, CARRYING OLIVE from in front of the Christmas tree, where the babysitter let her fall asleep in a nest of couch cushions, Erik throws out his back in a spectacular way. Definitely more than a tweak. The knifing pain from earlier in the taproom courses through his torso and into his thighs and groin like electroshocks. He crumples to the floor with his daughter in his arms and she wakes crying, affronted.

"What's going on," Amanda calls from the bathroom.

Erik hears Olive shout, "Daddy's dead!" and he can't correct her. Amanda comes running, which is nice, he thinks, through the white wall of agony that has risen up between him and his family.

Amanda sighs, gathers Olive into her arms. "Daddy's thrown his back out again. It happens to old men." Erik lies on the floor looking up at his wife and daughter conferring about his condition. He might as well be dead, that's how removed he feels. Amanda nudges him with her foot.

"Tylenol? Advil?"

He wants them to kneel down and kiss his brow, tell him it will be okay.

"Either," he groans. "Both."

"Are you just going to lie here?" Amanda says.

"I can't move."

She helps him get some pills down his throat and he falls asleep like that, on the floor between their bedrooms. When he wakes, he finds a duvet thrown over him. It's six a.m. He crawls along the hall, dragging the blanket with him, and makes his way down to the living room, takes the stairs one at a time on his ass. The berm outside their bare patio doors is dark except for a streetlight illuminating shaggy cedar limbs. Between their row of townhomes and the berm is a dead-end street. A modern-day miracle, Erik has always marvelled, to be living in the middle of the city on a quiet street with a woodland view: fir, maple, mountain ash. Once, walking with Olive, they'd spotted a barred owl in the branches overhead, another time a Cooper's hawk, a downy woodpecker. Amanda's right, though. The trees are dying, specifically the western red cedars. Over the past few years, Erik has watched them wither from the top down. City workers removed more than a dozen this past summer, and now there are gaps along the berm, more traffic noise from the artery on the south side seeping through.

Erik climbs onto the couch and thinks about the tent he can't see for the dark, the person inside whom his wife so vehemently wants gone. Erik doesn't exactly want him to stay, but he doesn't feel the same hostility toward the stranger. Maybe he's a young backpacker who's run out of money. A lost soul, down on his luck. Whatever the case, the situation demands empathy, doesn't it? Especially this time of year.

The next time he wakes, a bland morning light has entered the room. The pain in his back is curled like a sleeping animal—Erik pictures a wolverine—and he knows any movement will cause it to wake, snarling. The last time his back had revolted, he'd been unfurling a set of building plans. That's all. Pulling them from the cardboard tube and spreading them across his desk. Just prior to that he'd had a difficult conversation with a client, one of many with this particular individual who claimed his approach to homebuilding—which he knew nothing about—was rooted in his innate artistic sensibility. He had no artistic gifts that Erik could discern. He was an indecisive control freak. The project was over budget and behind schedule because of his waffling, and Erik held the stress of it in his back, apparently. His doctor had told him the seizing of discs wasn't caused only by physical exertions; they could be triggered by emotions. He could do all the yoga and swimming he wanted, but he should also heed the stress levels in his life before his body dealt with them on his behalf. What has he been ignoring to bring him to his knees, quite literally, this time? What is his body trying to tell him?

A slip of the lime-green nylon tent is visible now, through the trees, as well as a pair of legs standing beside it. Branches obscure the person's upper body, and smoke rises above where a head must be. It's hard for Erik to believe, but there'd been a time in his life, too, when a cigarette constituted breakfast. Around the same time, he'd had some struggles himself. An alarming pit of sadness had yawned open inside him where none had existed before. He'd almost fallen in—truthfully, he'd almost leapt. If it hadn't been for Amanda—who'd now been in his life longer than she hadn't—hauling him out for hikes, putting him to work around their ramshackle rental at the time, and basically refusing to let him be, he wasn't sure where he might have wound up.

HE NODS OFF AGAIN, and when he wakes a second time it's still two weekends before Christmas, the days stacked with parties and activities to get through, most of them arranged by Amanda. There's the Christmas train in Stanley Park, always on a miserable rainy night, and a visit to the mall Santa for the official photo of Olive with the imposter. There's a glittery staff party for the video game company where Amanda is a communications manager, held in the cavernous ballroom of a downtown hotel, and somewhere in there, a strata meeting

Erik will have to attend because Amanda finds them boring. Does she think he enjoys them? Erik can't remember the order in which these engagements are set to occur, but he knows they'll pop up like Whac-A-Moles he'll have to smack down to move forward. Move forward to what, though? The slump of January and the long wait until spring? Amanda is pushing for a weeklong vacation somewhere warm, but Erik doesn't see the point of just one week. He needs at least a month to decompress. When will they ever get a month? Amanda argues. She has a point. What he doesn't tell her is that he's also reacting against her impulse to do what all the other families around them are doing. The so-and-sos are going to Hawaii, the people-we-barely-know are taking the kids to Disneyland. Who cares? Do they even consider their carbon footprints? What's wrong with the local ski hills? What about storm watching in Tofino? Granted, Olive refuses to wear the bulky clothing required to spend any time in the snow, and there's nothing appealing about being cabin-bound on the west coast of Vancouver Island with a six-year-old while gale-force winds rage outside. Suffice to say, no vacation of any kind has been booked.

Today, Saturday, Erik opens his and Amanda's shared calendar and discovers the annual holiday strata meeting, complete with mulled wine and shortbread, scheduled for late afternoon.

"Please, no," Erik says from the couch where he still lies, parched.

"What now?" Amanda says. She's in the kitchen, slamming the coffee pot around, turning the taps on and off. Her voice is flat, angry. She only had two glasses, but she's probably hungover; the bubbly always slays her.

"I need to see a doctor."

"Breakfast!" Amanda calls lightly to Olive.

"Can you drive me?"

"I'll drop you off, but I don't want to wait there forever."

Erik sees dog-walkers beginning their morning march along the berm. The tent is set off the main footpath by a few metres, but anyone out walking will be able to see it clearly.

"Why don't you plug in the Christmas tree?" Amanda says.

"I'm a little—" Erik starts.

"I wasn't talking to you."

Erik hears his daughter's eager footsteps before she zooms into view, doing a knee-slide across the laminate floor and coming to a stop before the tree, naked as the day she was born.

AT THE STRATA MEETING, Erik feels no pain. The doctor has given him a few precious Valiums and a bottle of Tylenol 3s. He floats through the agenda and imagines sailing quite merrily through the rest of his evening.

"And, finally," the chairperson announces, "our last order of business before the holidays is to welcome our new neighbours, Ross and Leah."

A couple seated near the front of the room stands and waves to the crowd.

"Hi," Leah says. "We're really happy to have landed here."

"Yeah, what she said," Ross echoes bashfully.

So here they are, in the flesh, the couple whose private life Amanda so crudely exposed last night for the sake of conversation. Erik feels awkward knowing what he knows, what he supposedly knows, and grins all the more wildly to compensate.

"Welcome," he hears himself shout from the back of the room. Heads turn in his direction. He is definitely high. He knows he should leave it at that, but something about the attention now focused on him compels him to keep going. "We're an okay lot," he says. "We'll leave you be, or not. It's up to you." He chuckles. He has no idea what he's talking about. Then he adds, "Come by for a little Christmas cheer tonight, if you fancy. The wife would love to meet you." The wife! Amanda would murder him if she heard him refer to her as *the wife*. He might as well have called her *the old ball and chain*.

Leah and Ross nod, slowly lowering into their seats. He catches sight of himself then, his reflection in darkened glass: hair a bit wild given that he couldn't navigate the shower this morning, unshaved, rumpled flannel shirt, also unchanged since last night. He has a bit of a Cro-Magnon look going, but that isn't why they should be terrified. It's Amanda. Even if she isn't irked about his spontaneous invitation, or, he supposes, even if she is, she'll be compiling anecdotes and evidence as soon as they walk through the door, alert for any whiff of inuendo or injustice in their new neighbours' relationship. It will be her gossip to share, to dole out in whatever manner she chooses, and to whomever. What has Erik done? Practically invited lambs to the slaughter.

AMANDA IS SURPRISINGLY chill about Erik's hijacking of their evening. He would hazard to say she even perks up; lightness creeps into her voice, or irritation over his inconvenient injury leaks away.

"I doubt they'll come," she says, "but if they do, fine. Why not see what they're all about?"

"They're definitely coming. I told them seven o'clock and gave them our unit number." Erik's high is wearing off. He sits struggling to de-stem cilantro at the kitchen table.

"Did you invite anyone else?"

"Not that I recall."

Amanda laughs, a shimmering and authentic utterance. Erik's back unclenches and he takes the opportunity to draw a full breath.

"You know you're not supposed to drink on those pills," she says.

"Don't be such a downer," he says. "I get my kicks where I can."

"Fair enough," Amanda concedes. "Just don't get sloppy and leave me to be the adult."

"Oh, I plan on getting very sloppy."

"Fine. Me too, then. It'll be a race to the sloppiest." Amanda wears a half-grimace, half-grin as she slides the casserole dish of enchiladas into the oven. Erik is happy to be having what feels like a conversation with his wife, a fluid dialogue, anyway, without spiteful undercurrents.

"I wonder if they'll be the type to send a thank-you text. I always say, *Thanks for the great evening*, or *Last night was fun*."

Erik winces, partly from the ache that flowers suddenly at the base of his spine and begins to hug its way up his ribs, but mostly at Amanda's preemptive pettiness. "Are we going to cut them off if you don't get a courtesy note tomorrow?"

Amanda shrugs. "Gestures like that say a lot about people."

"What does it say about you?"

"That I have manners. That I appreciate the efforts of others."

"What if they say thanks in person? Do they have to do it again in writing?" Erik pushes the dish of cilantro aside with such force it almost skids off the table.

"Why're you getting all worked up about this?"

"You're the one making us entertain hypotheticals. We haven't even met them yet."

"It doesn't matter who they are. The same rules apply to everyone."

"It's just fake bullshit you're after."

"It's not bullshit. It's decent."

"It's harsh, Amanda. You're harsh," Erik says, or maybe he doesn't.

Later, after helping Olive into a party dress with actual blinking lights woven into it, Erik looks on his phone to see Amanda has posted a photo, a curated shot of the cocktail she was drinking while preparing dinner. In the photo: a glowing beeswax candle, ice cubes, spiced rum and oat-nog with a dusting of nutmeg. The caption reads: *Holiday fortification* ✔.

AT 7:10 P.M., Leah and Ross still haven't arrived. Erik considers the very real possibility that he didn't invite them, just mumbled something incomprehensible in their direction at the meeting, or, possibly, his invitation was for tomorrow, even next weekend. Who knows? He indulges a sense of relief at not having to entertain, dips into an alternate evening in which he eats an enchilada or two, takes a long, hot bath, and goes to bed with Olive, at eight o'clock. At 7:13 p.m., however, he hears the thunking arrival of feet on the outside steps, followed by a reticent knock on the door. Here they are. No mistake. *Buckle up*, Erik tells himself by way of encouragement from the couch where he lies entranced by the blinking lights on their hastily selected tree-lot varietal.

"Welcome," Erik hears Amanda say. "Glad you could make it on such short notice." Is that a dig for him to hear? Short notice translated as unapproved by her.

"Very kind," Erik hears another woman's voice say, soft, a little raspy. "Left the kids at home."

"Another time, then," Amanda says.

Erik recalls (miraculously, given his earlier condition) from the official welcome at the strata meeting that Ross and Leah's children are older, early teens. He's thankful not to have gotten Olive excited at the prospect of having new kids over; instead, Amanda thought to subdue her with a movie upstairs. Erik knows he should rise from the couch and match Amanda's graciousness, take Ross and Leah's coats, offer drinks, but he won't because Amanda herself has relegated him to this position, an invalid.

"Please, take your beverages to the living room and keep Erik company," he hears her say. "He's conveniently slipped a disc." There are laughs at his expense, at Amanda's humour, and that husky barroom singer's voice again, this time proffering sympathy: "Oh, how terrible," Leah says.

"Bring him this, will you?" Amanda says. "It'll make him feel included."

A few seconds later Leah stands before him with a glass of cherry-flavoured bubbly water.

"Do you want me to spike it with something?" she says.

"Bless you," he says. "But some karmic devilry has me enduring the darkest time of the year without alcohol. At least I have these." Erik takes the bottle of pills from his shirt pocket and gives them a shake. He has, in fact, just popped a couple to dull the pain and help him through the evening.

"Almost as good," she says.

"I'd offer you a seat on the couch—" Erik starts.

"There's plenty of room," Leah says. She sets her cocktail

on the coffee table, lifts his feet, and sits, placing them in her lap. Erik is momentarily stunned. His feet are suddenly resting in a strange woman's lap, and he is helpless to move them. This woman smells strongly of essential oils, the kind mothers in the neighbourhood are of late basting their children with, convinced of their abilities to cure any ailment or disorder, from a common cold to autism. Amanda had in fact recently attended a version of a Tupperware party but with tinctures of lavender, peppermint, and tea tree oils on offer. She came home with a selection, more out of obligation than any belief in their genuine healing properties, she claimed. It sounded like a gateway to anti-vax territory, Erik said; Amanda didn't argue.

Ross enters the living room then, and Erik feels even more awkward, caught in an act he did not commit. He tries to slide his feet from Leah's lap, but he only ends up wiggling his toes in his snowman-decorated socks.

"So, what's the verdict?" Erik says, trying to sound normal. "How are you two settling in to your new domicile?"

"So far, so good," Ross says, apparently unfazed by the picture of Erik and Leah sharing the couch.

"Shame about the neighbours, though, right, babe?" Leah says.

"Very funny," Erik says.

"Oh no, not you guys," Leah says, shaking his foot.

"That bum out there in the tent," Ross says, and jerks his head in the direction of the berm. Erik is struck by how quickly these two are rejecting his earlier impressions of them. At the strata meeting they'd given off a self-effacing, almost timid air. Here, in his home, they're aggressive, all swagger.

"*Bum*?" Amanda says, arriving before them with a glistening charcuterie board. "I think you mean *unhoused*."

"No," Ross says, "I most certainly do not." Amanda takes in Erik and Leah on the couch and subtly arches an eyebrow at him. Then she walks over to the patio doors and squints out into the darkness, the lashing rain. It's as though she's willing them to do the same. And they do. Their heads turn in the direction of outside, and for a moment they're silent, maybe recalling their own miserable camping experiences, because Erik's certain that's as close as any of them can come to understanding the situation beyond the warmth of the living room: a rained-out campsite they can, with relative ease, abandon and move to a hotel. Which is to say they can't understand at all.

"City's not doing anything about it," Leah says.

"I'm ready to deal with him myself," Ross says.

Erik recoils at Ross's vigilante-sounding bravado. He may sneer when he says, "Yeah? And how would you go about doing that?"

"Easy. Just huff and puff and blow the thing down."

Erik watches Leah nod her approval at his feet.

"Really?" he says to her.

"Imagine," she says.

"We don't have to, babe," Ross says. "We can do it tonight."

"Whoa, easy cowboy," Erik says. "Let's take the we out of this equation."

"Softy," Leah chides.

"It'll snow and he'll be gone," Amanda says matter-of-factly, as if this has been her stance all along, to wait the camper out.

"Maybe, maybe not," Ross says. "I'm more of a DIY guy."

"Oh really?" Amanda says, with what sounds like good-natured wonder, but simmers, Erik knows, with oily condescension. He sees, now, that her frustration over the camper has limits, that perhaps she's finally met that limit, right here in her own home. He wonders where she's going to go with this. He wants her to take it all the way like he knows she can. He wants her to take this whack job down.

"I have a pretty good track record for moving things along." Ross looks to Leah for confirmation.

"You do, babe," she says. "You get shit done." She covers her mouth primly, as if embarrassed about swearing. "These drinks," she says, wagging her glass at Amanda. "They're strong."

"Are they?" Amanda says. "I'd advise you to slow down, then. Don't want to expend our yuletide cheer too early in the evening."

"But they're so good," Leah says generously.

The timer beeps and Amanda leaves to pull the enchiladas from the oven.

"Wears the pants," Ross says, nodding in the direction of the kitchen.

"Excuse me?" Erik intends to say it sharply, but it comes out a drawl.

Ross smears an indecent amount of soft cheese on a cracker and places the entire thing in his mouth.

The word *douchebag* nudges against Erik's clenched teeth, but he swallows it with a hard gulp; Amanda wouldn't approve, though he's heard her use the insult in traffic.

"Look," Leah says, pointing in the direction of the berm, where a light can be seen leaping about in the darkness. A flashlight.

"He's home," Ross says. "How sweet."

The beam disappears inside the tent and illuminates the shape from within, dancing about before settling. What is the camper doing now? Erik wonders. Checking for leaks in the tent corners? Trying to warm himself in a sleeping bag? Does he even have one? That would be the thing to do, or one of the things to do; deliver something useful to the fellow. He could bring the guy an enchilada and a sleeping bag. Erik manoeuvres stiffly to an upright position. Ross drains his drink and slams the glass on the coffee table.

"You thinking what I'm thinking?"

"Doubt it," Erik says.

"Let's do this."

"Oh no. I definitely wasn't thinking that," Erik says.

"Got a flashlight?" Ross says.

"No, well, maybe in with the camping gear, but I—"

"Grab it. Let's go."

"Be careful," Leah says, looking at Erik. He blushes extravagantly and realizes that, in the mythology of Ross and Leah, it was never made clear who had been the adulterer. Erik had just assumed it was Ross, but something about Leah's focus on him since her arrival has upended that view. In his panic to escape her gaze, Erik finds himself digging through the camping bins in the crawlspace, no longer searching for a sleeping bag, as he'd originally thought he might, but preparing to accost the destitute stranger outside his home with his bully neighbour.

"What are you doing?" he hears Amanda hiss. She peers in at him, face flushed from cooking in their cramped kitchen, the potent drinks, and this bizarre turn with their company. He knows her face so well, and yet he doesn't know it at all. His back flutters a faint warning.

"The guy's obviously nuts," Erik says. "He's probably pro-wall and pro-life and whatever else. I can't believe I invited them over."

"You've never been a good judge of character," Amanda says.

"I was high." In fact, he still is.

"You're not actually going with him," Amanda says.

"I've got this," Erik says. The evening has run away from them, a speedboat without a driver, but Erik thinks he might be able to regain some control. Ross is a joke, a hulking doofus whose clumsy moves Erik should be able to predict.

"Really? Do you? Because from over here it looks like you're getting caught up in the madness." Her words give him pause. He looks at the open camping bins spewing gear, then back at Amanda, mascara melting beneath her eyes. He wants to fix this for her, for them.

"Trust me," he says,

"Yeah, sure." Amanda snorts. "By the way, the headlamps are hanging from that hook over there, where they always are. Have fun out there, cowboy."

She disappears from view, leaving a stink of disdain in her wake. He grabs the headlamps and stands for a moment, listening. It's as if someone has muted all conversation throughout the house; quiet pervades, except for the faint exuberance of Moana belting it out upstairs. Amanda doesn't understand. He might need to hold Ross back.

"If nothing else, I'm a witness," he says aloud to the bikes and tools and overwintering patio furniture. But even as he says it, he knows that by witness he means spectator, and by its very nature, a spectator is complicit. If called upon to act, to actually *do* something, will he? He doesn't have a fucking clue.

WHEN ERIK EMERGES from the crawlspace, he glances into the living room and sees Leah inspecting the decorations on his tree. Amanda is in the kitchen, banging dishware around unnecessarily. And Ross is waiting for him at the door. He snatches a headlamp from Erik and starts outside.

"Let's roll," he says, and Erik cringes at the implied heroics.

"Listen," Erik says, "don't pull any Rambo crap. We don't know anything about this guy."

"He might be a total psycho," Ross says. "Can I pull my Rambo crap if he is?"

Erik feels a dull tweak in his back and falls behind Ross as he weighs the severity of the pain. He walks tentatively, rain quickly soaking his hair and sliding down his shirt collar; he forgot to grab a jacket but can't turn back now. They leave the enclave and cross over to the chip path that leads steeply up onto the berm. Erik can't think of anything he'd rather be doing less, anyone he'd rather be doing it with. As they plod along the path, he looks through the trees and the gaps where trees stood until recently, back to the row of townhomes, his row, aglow with strings of coloured lights. In a couple homes, other festive gatherings are underway and Erik is envious of how drunkenly straightforward their evenings are no doubt unfolding.

As they approach the tent site, Erik purposely slows his stride. He needs to understand what's happening in real time and intervene at the right moment. Or maybe he should just wrestle Ross to the ground now. Their commotion will alert the camper. Erik can destroy the element of surprise Ross is so villainously counting on. Up ahead, Ross stops on the footpath, waiting for him. Having turned off his headlamp, he's a dark shape, a hulking outline. There's no way Erik could subdue him, not in his fragile state.

"Ready?" Ross says in a loud whisper.

"No," Erik says, keeping his voice at a hush. If he spoke in a regular voice, or if he yelled, he could quash this ambush in its tracks. Why doesn't he?

A few metres down the trail, the tent glows softly, a green orb in the dark, alien and unknown. Erik hears a burst of coughing from inside, followed by phlegmy throat clearing. The dude is unwell. They're about to attack a sick, homeless man. Ross stalks the perimeter of the tent. Erik clears his throat, too, but it comes out sounding more like a gasp.

He realizes they're now parallel with his home and he can see his patio, the string of lights he dutifully looped around his own railing in a tired attempt at holiday spirit. He hears a shout then—"What the fuck?"—and sees Ross ripping the fly from the tent. As Erik runs forward, the beam from his headlamp strobing across tree trunks, he catches sight of details he couldn't have discerned from his deck: a carefully woven fence constructed of windfall, possibly built to shield the tent from view of dog-walkers, or as a buffer from the winds that rise over the south side of the berm; a flat rock on which a pot, a mug, and one spoon are arranged.

"You're done," Ross says. "Squatter's paradise ends now."

Erik tries to wrest the fly from Ross's grip. Maybe he can drape it back over the tent and they can leave as if nothing happened. But Ross isn't budging. He holds firm and uses the slippery fabric to whip Erik backwards in what might look like a choreographed dance move, the way Erik reels with a flourish, still holding onto the fly until the last moment when, at full extension, he jerks off and plunges toward the ground. As he falls—even before he hits the earth, and through his Valium haze—he feels his back seizing in anticipation of the impact. It's going to be bad; he'll likely have to be carried out of here on a stretcher. Some witness. All he sees is blackness as he falls face first to the earth.

"The fuck you doing?" Erik hears a man's voice—not his own, though it could be—high-pitched and panicked. He rolls onto his side to see Ross pulling up the tent pegs, the green orb imploding. The camper scrambles out before his shelter is completely flattened, and for a moment their eyes meet. Erik sees himself in his early twenties, lost and inexplicably sad. He avoids reflecting on this period of his life, but now, without warning, he's looking it in the eye.

"Is everyone okay?" he hears Amanda call from the deck. "What's going on over there?"

Why don't you get over here and see for yourself, Erik wants to shout back. Make it an Instagram story while you're at it. You can caption it: Just your average Christmas party, chasing off the disadvantaged! But he can't speak. The words jam in his throat. His body is shutting down, protesting.

Ross has flattened the tent and now reaches inside, pulls the man's effects out into the rain: backpack, blanket, food containers.

"Jesus, man!" the camper squawks from somewhere nearby. "Leave my shit alone."

"Your shit's gotta go," Ross says. "This isn't a fucking campground."

"Does it look like I'm here for a good time?" the guy says.

"It *looks* like you're bringing down my property value," Ross says. He starts gathering the tent into a crude roll.

"Fucking drop it," the guy says. "I'll go."

Ross flings the balled-up nylon into some bushes. Then he starts on the backpack, extracting items of clothing and flinging them about in the dark.

Erik has to do something. He groans onto his stomach and tries to communicate instructions to his right arm. Kindly, it responds. He lifts himself up onto his elbow and uses it to drag himself forward, the way Olive got around instead of crawling. He inches through the wet dirt, rich with the smells of minerals and decaying leaves. Ross mutters under his breath, words Erik can't make out. Then he begins to whistle. Whistle? Seriously? Who is this sadist, now his neighbour, whom he'd actually invited into his home? Erik thrusts his elbow forward with more gusto, again and again, until he's eye-level with Ross's ankles. He needs to make his next move count because he won't get a second chance. He rears up like a cobra, then strikes, biting Ross's calf where it meets his Achilles tendon. In the split second before Ross registers the pain, Erik wraps his right arm around Ross's ankles and jerks them tightly together. When Ross attempts to spin around, he topples. It's a perfectly executed combination of moves.

"Fucker!" Ross yells. "Sympathizer!" He boots Erik in the head as he struggles free of his ankle-hold.

Despite some dizziness, Erik feels energized; he's more than a bystander, and, to his relief, he's not an accomplice. He can hear the camper's heavy breathing close by as he grabs his backpack and other strewn items.

"Hurry," Erik moans. But to what, and where? The guy has nowhere to go.

"Mission complete," Ross says, standing to kick over the camper's meagre kitchen supplies. He leaves Erik lying in the dirt and lunges down the berm onto the street.

Erik pushes himself up to sit. Despite the gauzy chemical cocktail buffering his pain receptors, his whole body is ablaze. The camper has run off into the night and Erik knows he won't be back.

"It's done!" Ross shouts to the women on the deck.

"You're a special kind of nightmare, aren't you," Amanda calls back. Erik thinks she slurs her words. Leah appears moments later, running down the street toward Ross with an umbrella. It's Olive's umbrella, patterned with pink flamingos, presumably taken from Erik's front porch. When she reaches Ross, she holds it over his head, as if to protect the muddied brute from a few raindrops. He swoops her into an embrace. It's too much. Erik must now encounter these nutcases daily, in the recycling room, in the parking garage.

"Hey!" he shouts. "That's my kid's umbrella."

Leah looks up from beneath the streetlamp toward the

berm, searching, but he's invisible to her, shielded by the sheeting rain and mesh of branches.

"And you'll get it back," she snaps. "We're neighbours, aren't we?"

Acknowledgements

Thank you to my agent, Samantha Haywood, for championing this collection to publishers and for her guidance.

Thank you to House of Anansi for continuing to celebrate and elevate short stories, and to the entire team for their thoughtful production on all levels, from proofreading to design. Thank you, especially, to my dear friend and editor, Shirarose Wilensky. So many good things begin on Granville Island.

Thank you to my Good Art Friends, Théodora Armstrong, Anna Ling Kaye, and Doretta Lau, for their insights, conversations, and always a laugh. I'm fortunate to have such incredibly smart readers as friends.

Earlier versions of some of the stories in this book appeared in literary magazines: "In Loco Parentis" in *The Fiddlehead*; "Hyacinth" and "Nest" in *The New Quarterly*; and "Weekend Guest" in *Prairie Fire*. Thank you to the editors of these magazines. Thank you also to Steven W. Beattie for selecting "Nest" for inclusion in *Best Canadian Stories 2025*.

I'm grateful to the Canada Council for the Arts for the financial support in writing this book.

Thank you, always and forever, to my parents, Patricia and Terence, for instilling in me a love of reading and writing and encouraging me to play with words and make things up.

Cole and Jude—you are my perfect home. Thank you for this evolving life.

© Taylor Sandham

CLEA YOUNG's stories have been included in numerous literary journals, three volumes of *The Journey Prize Stories*, and *Best Canadian Stories 2025*. She has twice been longlisted for the CBC Short Story Prize. Her debut story collection, *Teardown*, was published by Freehand Books. Young grew up in Victoria, BC, and completed an MFA at the University of British Columbia. She lives in Squamish, BC.